Let Me Carry You

Karen Tucci

True Heart Romance

Dedication

♥

To my Aunt Carole and Uncle Walter "Bupo" Charowsky:

"To know you is to love you." Through research, I discovered that Bobby Vinton had a song with that title in 1969, which I imagine you knew. Those words ring true for both of you. It's not very often one can find two caring, generous, and loving people married to each other, yet I have the best example in both of you! Andrea, the main character in the story, was inspired by you, Aunt Carole. Though you were disabled with Multiple Sclerosis, you had the same fiery passion and "Go Get 'em" attitude as her. And Uncle Bupo, you inspired Brent's character. You were a loving, doting man who'd carry his woman anywhere. For decades, your devotion to Aunt Carole was admirable and not easily found nowadays.

I love and miss you both. Thank you for being classy role models to follow.

R.I.P.

Contents

Karen's Other Books:

Stand Alone Books:

<u>When the Dust Settles: A Sweet Romance with a Navy SEAL</u>

G & G Security Series (Coming 2025)

(The characters from When the Dust Settles cross-over in this series)

Operation: Heal my SEAL Book 1

Operation: Find my SEAL Book 2

Operation: Keep my SEAL Book 3

Operation: Train my SEAL Book 4

Second Chance Series:

<u>Starting Over</u>

<u>Moving On</u>

Big L' Ranch Series

<u>The Perfect Kiss: Book 1</u>

<u>The Perfect: Cowboy Book 2</u>
<u>The Perfect Match Book 3</u>
<u>The Perfect Christmas (Holiday Novella)</u>
<u>The Perfect Sheriff Book 5</u>

Best Friends Series
<u>Let Me Carry You</u>
<u>Let Me Marry You</u>

YA Cumberland Christian Prep School Series
The Big Score (Coming 2025)

Chapter 1

♥

*T*WO MORE RUNGS! ANDREA thought as her arms and shoulders trembled. Her leg muscles surely would be, too, but feeling anything below the waist disappeared right after the accident. Andrea knew her wheelchair was waiting for her at the exit like an angry parent welcoming their child home an hour after curfew.

If I dropped the rope, the attendant said the harness would catch me - it's safe. Those two words ran through Andrea's head like a hamster on a wheel. Is anything safe anymore? She was in this world without any family and, to top it all off, confined to a chair.

Andrea heard Donna, the most supportive best friend in the world, yelling encouraging words from the platform behind her, but Andrea's ultra-focus honed in on reaching the T-bar.

Even though Donna had told Andrea to go to an adaptive course first, Andrea refused. Despite her best friend's severe fear of heights, Donna wouldn't let Andrea face this new challenge alone. For that, Andrea loved her.

Burn Baby Burn! Andrea thought her triceps would pop right out of her arm as she yanked herself up the next rung. She'd heard before that burning doesn't show weakness; it shows growth and strength. Given that, Andrea had to be stronger than Sampson right now! Three more rungs and the ropes supervisor would help her to the platform, where she would zip line through the trees to her awaiting prison on wheels.

Before her accident, Andrea had been a runner. She had strong quad muscles. In fact, they were so strong a doctor had told her once that she had leg strength that many men dreamed they could. Now, much of that strength and definition had disappeared after five hundred forty-nine days of living in a chair.

Andrea refused to let her desire for adventure disappear like her leg muscles, even though the owner of this establishment tried to prevent her from coming today. He hadn't even seemed impressed that she'd worked here as a teen. Dave, the previous owner, and her dad had been friends. Her record for completing each course one hundred times in one summer when she was fourteen hadn't fazed him either.

This man obviously had no soul. He sounded relatively young, but he was probably one of those men who had a radio voice - intriguing and young sounding - yet when given the opportunity to see a picture of the radio man, he appeared twenty years older than you thought, and he had the furniture disease - where his chest had dropped into his drawers!

After sharing her experience and a clear representation of her ability to handle the zip lines here, he congratulated her on her accolades right before he said, '*That was when you were able to walk.*' The nerve. Evidently, he hadn't listened to her explain her experience since she'd been in this prison on wheels. *Focus!* She scolded herself for letting that jerk's words invade her.

I cannot quit. I'll show him, not able to walk, whatever! Laser-focused on the last rung, she bore down deep and blared, "I will rise from the ashes!"

With one final swing and grunt, Andrea reached the tower platform and collapsed, arms spread wide, eyes closed, and rapid, shallow breathing. Moments later, Andrea took a deep breath and propped herself on her elbows as every muscle she could feel screamed obscenities at her.

The ropes supervisor gently touched her shoulder, "May I pick you up and move you to the other side of the platform?" That would have been the easiest way to get her there. She didn't doubt his ability, given his shoulders that looked like he majored in rowing.

No matter how much she appreciated the trepidatious college-aged supervisor's offer to help, Andrea refused to accept any in case it got back to the owner of this establishment. If she had to see a smug look on his face...

Frustration filled her entire body, just uttering the thought.

"I'm going to scoot back and swing my legs around." Andrea sounded strong, but her body felt like Popeye without his spinach.

"No worries. He knew you wouldn't accept any help."

"Excuse me?" Andrea deadpanned. She stared as the employee's eyes widened like he revealed a secret.

"Um...I...he shared your determination."

She knew that was a nice way of saying she was difficult to deal with. That ticked her off even more. *She didn't want or need any help; if she did, she'd ask.* Well, she wouldn't, but that was beside the point. Maybe when she reached the end of the zip line, she'd tell the owner a thing or two about professionalism. In the meantime, Andrea set her mind on finishing this course.

The attendant remained on guard and held his hands in the ready position but let her move herself. Andrea appreciated this thoughtfulness and preparedness. It wasn't him who'd caused her frustration. On the contrary, he'd been encouraging her since she and Donna started the course, and now he was a vigilant spotter.

Urg! Focus. Don't let him distract you, but don't kill yourself either. If you need help, ask! Where did that voice come from? Andrea knew that she had to focus. Given her exhaustion and lack of leg function, she could get hurt if she continued to worry about the jerkface owner.

After scooting backward, Andrea placed her arms on the seat of a chair the attendant had in place for her. As she pulled herself up, her arm muscles were shaking. The attendant quickly placed his hands under her legs and gave her a little nudge back onto the seat, then moved away quickly, probably hoping to avoid any argument that might ensue because he assisted her, Andrea surmised.

Glancing at the attendant's name tag, Andrea whispered, "Thank you, Steve." She felt a little defeated but highly appreciative.

"It was nothing." Steve stared at her, looking apprehensive.

"What's wrong?" Andrea's voice, shaky.

"I need to lift you for the hook to attach to the zip line. He stared at her, probably waiting for her to speak. She hated that his boss put it in his head that she was a difficult person to deal with. No wonder she hadn't seen him today. Besides being a complete nincompoop, he was a coward, too. Telling his employees lies about her and then hiding away somewhere. Pshaw!

Andrea had recognized the problem herself. "I need to be higher, don't I?" The attendant just nodded his head.

"I'm sorry you have to lift me." She frowned and spread her arms wide, waiting for the attendant to do his thing. At this moment, Andrea felt vulnerable. Thankfully, Donna showed up just in time to put a smile on her face.

"Ah, you did let someone help you." Donna's spit out breathlessly.

As Steve placed the ball of his foot on Andrea's chair, one hand around her back and the other under her thighs, he picked her up like she weighed nothing, propping her on his thigh. Steve grabbed her hook and latched it on the half-inch thick cord. Then he continued, "Just for the record, I don't mind helping you. I admire you." Andrea could only manage a meek smile as Steve tugged on the hook, a safety check required every time a patron latched onto a new section of the course. He got her ready to glide back to the ground. "Ready?"

Andrea grabbed the T-bar, flashed Steve a smile, and nodded. The attendant lifted her off his knee in one quick swoop and let her go. As Andrea sailed quickly through trees, she embraced the sensation and excitement rushing through her veins. She hadn't felt this alive since before her accident. Andrea extended her arms and soared like the lead duck in a V formation. She didn't want this to stop. This rip-roaring ride gave her some freedom back that she'd lost. Ever since the accident, her chair had imprisoned her. She enjoyed this jailbreak! More importantly, she didn't want to stop physically because she didn't know how she would. Before the accident, she had always dropped onto a cargo net, bounced a few times in a seated position, and rolled off onto the ground. All of that, of course, had involved using her legs. Like a brick smacking her in the face, she remembered all too well that her legs could no longer be counted on, and her heart longed for the times before her accident.

Peering through the trees, Andrea spied a tall, dark-haired man moving toward the side of the cargo net, and despite the distance, the burly man stole her eye's attention. As Andrea approached the zip line's end, she heard him barking out orders.

"Turn backward. Brace for impact."

That voice sounded irritatingly familiar to Andrea, and then, *Wham!* Her back slammed against the mat the owner had demanded be put in place just for her. *That stung!* Andrea could tell she was heading for that pad again, but at a significantly slower pace, and she tightened every capable muscle in her body, hoping it didn't feel like the first jolt.

Andrea squeezed her eyes shut, waiting for the bang. *Thump!* Instead of an unforgiving jolt from the hard mat, as she had felt during the first slam that had sailed her back five feet, she felt a more organic hardness that gripped her and wouldn't let go. She opened her eyes and slowly let out the breath she hadn't realized she'd been holding. Without thinking, she placed her arm around this hunk of a man's neck who spun her sideways, preparing to carry her off the cargo net. Time seemed to stand still as they locked eyes with each other. Andrea could feel his massive biceps enveloping her body. She shivered. Funny, she hadn't felt like this when Steve, her *'I can't be with you Andrea because you don't walk anymore ex-boyfriend,'* picked her up. Even the cool breeze welcoming autumn early into this beautiful New England town hadn't bothered her.

She hadn't felt trembled like that...ever. Andrea burdened her brain to think of a time when Kyle had ever made her shiver. She could only recall disgust, anger, and annoyance, but he never made her feel alive with his touch.

Andrea must have looked ridiculous, with loose, sweaty tendrils of light brown hair protruding from her ponytail and dirt-stained clothes. She stared at this well-defined, chiseled man like a deer in the headlight. His ruffled, jet-black hair had a little length on top but not below the ears. *Would his hair feel silky?* Her gaze halted on...

Those lips! *They look* just puffy enough to kiss.

What!? Get a grip! Where is this coming from? The last year-and-a-half of isolating herself seemed to be catching up with her. Andrea took a deep breath, licked her lips, and swallowed to bestow moisture in her dry mouth.

"Do you need water? Are you okay? The name tag he sported read Brent in large letters, and underneath it stated: Owner/Operator. The familiarity of his voice came rushing back. The tense phone conversations, his demeaning words, his pigheaded remarks. *Dear God, get this man away from me.* No wonder Andrea had been irritated by his voice barking orders at her.

Brent *definitely* didn't match the description of her imaginary radio guy. He may have the radio voice, but she had never imagined for a second that he would look like the epitome of a beautifully sculpted Greek god. Now that he wasn't barking orders at her or arguing with her on the phone, his voice sounded even more sultry and romantic.

Get a grip! She chastised herself again. *He just asked if I was okay. He didn't ask to marry me. As if that's ever going to happen...now. No one wants a broken woman.*

"Andrea!" Brent broke through her thoughts. "I need to get you out of the way. Can you release the safety clip?" Brent's voice was gruff.

Andrea's eyes traveled over his massive, broad shoulders and well-ripped chest. The collared, tight-fitted polo revealed the ripples in his upper abs and 3D peck muscles. *Ooh la la.*

*Why bother getting excited? I'll never date again, especially someone who owns this place and looks like that. He has *four working limbs, and clearly, he uses them all the time and in all the right ways.* Andrea shook her head, free of any more dangerous thoughts.

Then, Andrea recalled his words that had eaten away at her soul since the moment he uttered them. '*That was when you could walk'.* Andrea's demeanor changed quickly. She pushed off one of his shoulders, trying to wriggle out of his hold, "Just put me down and bring my chair...please. I'll scoot—."

"—Ahhh. Andrea, I'm going to kill you."

A smile filled her face. She knew that voice anywhere. Donna wanted to be happier about zip-lining, but her fear of heights had gotten the best of her by the sounds of it.

Before she knew what was happening, Brent had un-latched her hook and, in one fluid motion, placed his arm back underneath her legs like a husband carries his wife over the threshold and spun her around to her awaiting chair.

Exasperated by the situation, Andrea lashed out. "I could have made it here myself. I didn't need you to plop me like a sack of potatoes."

"I think a sack of potatoes is a bit of an exaggeration. If you had undone the hook when I asked and not tried to hop out of my arms..." He froze, wide-eyed. "I mean, fall out of my arms, then I wouldn't have had to move so quickly. Nonetheless, I am sorry if I hurt you or anything."

His apology surprised her. For the last month and a half, he'd been stubborn and refused to listen to her. While he started that way today, he'd also expressed regret. She even noticed his correction in words. *Yeah, I know I can't hop anywhere. Fall? Yes, I can do that just fine.*

"I accept your apology. Thank you. His sincerity showed on his face. It filled Andrea with an unfamiliar warmth in her chest. Could this guy be as bad as she thought he was?

Chapter 2

♥

ANDREA HAD SQUEALED AS she gripped his shoulders tighter. Brent couldn't tell if it was a good or lousy squeal. He hoped to avoid another disagreement with his guest. Given her gruff demeanor, he'd never expected her to be so easy on the eyes.

Er, hello, where did that come from? This is the pushy woman I dreaded getting a call from. Stop thinking of her like that. It makes sense, though the pushy ones are always beautiful on the outside.

After putting Andrea down in her chair, he stepped aside, trying to put as much space as possible between the two of them so maybe, just maybe, the feel of her soft skin and cottony ocean shampoo or body wash fragrance would dissipate from his internal senses. He wasn't supposed to be noticing her scent; *what the heck!* That scent had made his knees buckle for a brief moment. He steadied himself on the arm of her chair. His fingers brushed against her forearm, sending an electric current to his brain. He noted how quickly Andrea jerked away. *She must still hate me. I have to make sure everyone stays safe here. She had the craziest ideas that would have put her, and everyone else, in danger...* Brent vowed to protect people when they came to his establishment. He refused to lose another person on his watch.

Without Brent's assistance, Andrea hadn't stood a chance at disembarking from the zip line, whether she would admit that was another story. He had told her this multiple times in the last few weeks, but she insisted she could do it on her own. Finally, at the beginning of this week, he presented her with a compromise. Either he would have a minimal role in getting her off the zip line, or he would refund her money, and she would not be able to participate. Now that Brent's retinas were burned with this woman's beautiful ocean-green eyes, he was glad she had taken the deal.

Just then, Andrea's smile caught Brent's attention as she cheered and hollered for her friend. She unhooked from the zip line and bounced onto the cargo net.

Brent had never imagined this woman could smile or be heart-stoppingly beautiful. Brent liked Andrea's smile with her naturally straight, white teeth. His only interaction with the woman resulted in seeing her dark, bitter, angry side. Before today, he'd thought all Andrea needed was a *'beware of the dog'* sign chained around her neck to match her personality. Now, he knew that using the word dog and Andrea in the same sentence was a sin.

It'd been a long time since Brent focused on anything other than work. Two seasons ago, after graduating with his business degree, Brent had bought Adventure Park. Dave had run this park for the better part of forty years. He and his wife, Shirley, were tired and had no children to continue their legacy. Though Dave had mentioned a woman he thought of as his daughter taking it over, she had experienced hard luck and didn't want to purchase the business after all.

Emotion threatened to choke Brent. He knew all too well how a bad experience could change a person's life. He'd hoped the new business responsibilities would keep his mind off the fact that he was a murderer. That might be a little harsh. Brent convinced himself over the years that charges would have been downgraded to manslaughter if it had been brought to court. Fortunately for Brent, Dave understood his need to go all in.

"It was an accident," his parents and Joe had told him repeatedly. Maybe he knew that on some level, but he'd taken the blame for the entire situation in his conscious state.

This business had been his lifeline. Joe, the man next to him, had been like a brother to him since kindergarten and now he got to call him a business partner, too. Then annoyance filled him as he thought about the stress Andrea had caused him and the wedge she'd driven between him and Joe, all because Brent wanted to keep her safe. Joe had sided with her, saying that she had the experience and we should let her try it because it was a good business plan: work on adaptations for disabled people who still want to be active.

He'd never forget her words, *"I'm not trying to be difficult..." yeah, right.* This woman had difficulty written all over her snugly at the top but loose around the waist, dri-fit, orange tee shirt, and royal blue leggings.

If he weren't careful, her shiny hair that hung loosely at the nape of her neck with many curly tendrils cascading down the front of her body would blind him from seeing the beast underneath.

Brent crossed his arms over his chest and scoffed to himself. He didn't want to get involved with another woman, especially one as beautiful as Andrea. *She'll just end up breaking my heart, and who knows, I'd probably kill her too, or both if history repeats itself.*

He turned his attention back to the here and now. Donna rolled off the net, a little disoriented. She crawled over to Andrea's chair, pulled herself up, breathless, and declared, "I will never do anything like this again, my dear, lovely friend. We need to find you someone to go on adventures with because it is not me." She then collapsed on her back, arms stretched out and unwilling to move, regardless of what could happen being that close to the cargo net.

Brent and Joe stifled laughs until they couldn't refrain any longer. At which point, Andrea shot daggers at both of them. Brent slapped Joe's chest with the back of his hand and motioned his head toward Donna.

In three strides, Joe was at the woman's side. Brent knew that look in his friend's eyes. Joe had eyes for the collapsed woman. Donna propped herself up, staring at Joe, then Andrea. The awkward silence made Andrea smile. There it was again, that smile. Brent's stomach quivered. What were the women trying to say to each other without speaking?

Watching the interaction between Joe and Andrea's friend was torture. Joe shrugged his shoulders as he stared longingly at Donna. "You'll get used to it." Donna pulled her elbows from underneath herself and plopped back down on the ground. Joe cupped his hands, one on top of the other, placing them under her head before it whacked off the unforgiving earth. *Thank goodness. He probably saved us a lawsuit.* If Donna had hurt herself, Andrea wouldn't have let it go.

Brent's chest deflated when he watched Andrea storm away, small billows of dust leaving a trail behind her wheels. Her arm's triceps bulged as she rolled away like she was trying to win a wheelchair race. Donna had to jog to keep up with her.

Oh well.

Her fierceness irritated him. Even more annoying, for a brief second, he imagined trailing his fingertips up and down her toned arms. What didn't she understand? He was trying to help her stay alive and avoid another injury when her friend came barreling down at thirty miles per hour. *Weren't women supposed to like it when men protected them? Maybe she was more upset that her friend suggested that I be the one to take her on some adventures.* The daggers she'd shot her friend had made him cringe. Perhaps she didn't like how Joe and her friend were getting along so chummy. It hadn't helped that Steve had let it slip about his little warning at the morning meeting. That had given her one more thing to be mad at him for.

Good Riddance! Brent's jaw hardened. *Why were the pretty ones always so frustrating?*

Nope. Brent didn't mean that. He refused to think about twisting a finger around her light brown, bouncy curls that stretched down her back and over her shoulders in the front when she released her hair from the slagging ponytail. Nor would he remember the whiff of her perfume or whatever it was that smacked him in the face, taking up permanent residence in his nostrils. She smelled like a beach - one of his favorite places.

Man, she smelled heavenly.

Brent couldn't tell exactly what her deep green eyes had been saying, but man, they had looked mesmerized for one minute, unable to take them off him. *Was she checking me out? Did she like what she saw?* He wasn't fixated on keeping himself in shape; it just happened with this lifestyle. He lifted three times a week, but everything else came from hiking, running, swimming, climbing, skiing, and surfing. There wasn't a sport he wouldn't try.

But then, the next minute, her eyes had been trying to bore a hole through him. Brent convinced himself that experiencing any adventures with Andrea would set him up for disappointment and regret. He had sworn off women after his last relationship, if that's what you'd call it. It's a good thing he and Andrea didn't like each other. She could have made his life difficult.

"Brent? Brent? Earth to Brent!" Joe smacked Brent in the chest with a towel at closing time. "Did you hear a word I said?"

"No, sorry. What's up, Bud?"

"What's on your mind? Rather, who's on your mind? A beautiful brunette with arms that could take you, okay, me down in an arm wrestling match in seconds." Joe teased his best bud.

Without hesitating, Brent socked Joe in the arm. Andrea wasn't buff, just toned. Her arms were well-shaped but still attractive. He'd keep that thought to himself. "Are you ready to get out of here?" he asked, shaking more images of Andrea out of his head.

"You can't just change the subject. Joe countered.

Urg, Joe wouldn't stop until Brent gave him something. "Andrea is a beautiful woman - physically - but her attitude is worse than sour grapes before fermentation." Brent lifted one side of his mouth and shook his head.

Joe slapped him on the upper back. "Don't you think she's trying to adjust to being in a chair? Imagine how you would be if you were suddenly unable to do what you wanted." Joe straightened out the merchandise on the shelf nearest him. "You would be trying things you knew were physically impossible. You'd probably kill yourself trying to prove a point to yourself and everyone else." A smirk grew on his face. "Besides, aren't feisty ones the most fun?" He waggled his eyes at Brent.

A thunderous roar burst from Brent. Joe's animation could always make him laugh. He hated it when Joe made valid points. He didn't know anything about this woman's past, but based on what he had seen today, Brent pictured an athletic, always on-the-move person who'd enjoyed life by challenging her body with many endeavors. That didn't excuse her behavior.

"When did you become Dr. Phil?" Brent asked smartly.

A knock came at the glass door, stealing both men's attention. "Ohh, the beautiful, non-adventurous blonde from earlier," Joe rushed to the door.

"Who's got someone on his mind? Brent bantered.

Joe unlocked the door and stepped aside, "Donna, right?" Joe acted like he didn't know her name. Brent knew better. He turned his back to prevent her from seeing his grin. Joe hadn't stopped rambling about Donna since they'd left earlier. After that, Brent had spent the better part of his day letting Joe know he couldn't use business information to get her phone number.

"Hi, ya." Brent barely heard Donna's faint whisper. She stared hopelessly at Joe for who knows how long. Brent found this painful. Two shy people were trying to communicate. *Oh, brother.*

Stifling his smirk, Brent strolled out from behind the counter, trying to prevent Joe from reliving the day back in junior high when he'd tried to talk to Melissa Kennedy, *the prettiest girl on the face of the earth,* according to Joe. Instead of seizing his opportunity, he tripped over his words until another boy strolled up, taking her attention away.

"Is there something we can help you with?" Brent tried to speed up this awkward encounter between the two speechless adults, interfering with his ability to go home, get dinner, and watch the game.

Breaking her gaze with Joe, she turned to Brent and apologized for Andrea's behavior earlier.

"Does she know you're here? Brent questioned.

"No." Donna shook her head.

"I didn't think so. Has that woman ever apologized?"

Donna smiled understandingly. "Give her a break; she's come a long way. Andrea never used to get grumpy, but now she's just so vulnerable." Donna shrugged her shoulders. "I'll deny I said that if you repeat it." She laughed at the widely overused statement.

Brent nodded, showing his understanding.

"I will always defend Andrea because I know she has a kind, gentle, humble disposition, at least she had before the accident. I've noticed a change in Andrea lately, but I hope I can help my best friend find her true self again by intervening. She needs more time to adjust to her new way of life."

Brent wondered if Donna was trying to sell him on the fact that her friend was more than a grumpy, bitter, young woman. What did she mean by intervening?

She was dead wrong if Donna thought she could set Andrea up with him. He wasn't looking to date anyone, especially a stubborn woman who felt she had something to prove to everyone around her.

"How long has it been?" Brent inquired.

"February twenty-first will be two years." Donna's voice filled with sympathy.

"What happened?" Brent surprised himself. Why did he keep asking questions? He didn't need to know more. He needed to go home and watch the game.

"That's not my story to tell, but maybe she'll tell you sometime."

Brent let out a belly laugh. "Not likely, given the way she stormed out of here. She would have rather been knocked out by you and wished I didn't exist."

Checking the glass cases to ensure they were locked, Brent used it as a ploy to get the woman to leave or talk with Joe. It worked.

Brent could only hear whispering, which didn't settle well with him. Returning to the seemingly cozy, new couple, Brent tried to speed this meeting along.

"Well, I wasn't kidding when I said she had to find someone else to go on adventures with because I am not suited for what she likes. Not yet, anyway. I don't desire the rush, thrill, or excitement like she does. She won't do the adaptive outings, so I need you guys to help me," Donna pleaded.

Brent shifted back and forth, anxious about where this was going. He shook his head and strode back to the safety of his counter. Donna followed Brent, and Joe trailed Donna like a lost puppy dog, looking for someone to feed him.

"Here's what I was thinking." Donna stopped abruptly at the counter, not crossing behind. Seeing that she understood this was his business and respected boundaries was excellent. After that brief pause, Donna forged ahead with her idea, giving Brent an ache at the base of his head. "I'm meeting Andrea at Guido's Italian restaurant in an hour for dinner - it's her favorite place to eat and—"

"—I see where this is headed," Brent murmured, cutting her off. He wasn't going on a date with the woman who had strolled out of here hours earlier with venom oozing from her fangs, ready to sink into Brent's vulnerable flesh.

Donna smiled and shrugged her shoulders, still inviting them with her eyes, not her words, until she noticed Brent not budging. "You and Joe could just be having a drink at the bar, and then we come in, and I ask you guys to join us."

Brent shared a look with Joe, who'd moved behind Donna, and shook his head so vigorously that Brent thought his friend might get whiplash. "I have an idea," Brent began, "why doesn't Joe be the pawn in your little plan? I'll go home and watch the game."

Undiscouraged, Donna tried to argue the point despite the annoyance in his voice. "If you just—"

"—I don't think this is a good idea. She cannot stand me, remember?" Brent slapped a hand down on the counter harder than he meant to and quickly brushed that same hand through his hair. He wanted to keep his distance from Andrea.

Donna squared her shoulders, stood slightly taller, and continued, "It seems you're just as much a coward as Andrea. You both deserve to be alone."

"I see why you're friends. What happens when you're both feisty at the same time?" He should call her bluff and let her walk right out the door. It'd been too long since he'd even been interested in a woman, let alone on a date with one. He couldn't imagine trying to converse with one as dynamic as Andrea.

Joe sidled up to the counter, directly in front of Brent, talking to his friend with his eyes, asking him to go. Brent knew it was so that he could get to know Donna. Then, a thought struck Brent. "This sounds just like dinner. How is this doing *you* a favor?"

Donna sucked in a deep breath and let it out. "Andrea wants to go hiking in a few months when the foliage is beautiful. Of course, there isn't any place more beautiful than New England in the fall, but she can't physically complete the Mountain of Death."

Both the men looked puzzled.

"Oh, sorry, that's how I refer to the Knife's Edge.

"Mount Katahdin," both men said in unison and then punched each other in the shoulder like some juvenile ritual they've had for a long time when they spoke the same word simultaneously. Donna raised her eyebrows and smiled at Joe. Impressively, Joe hadn't flinched, even though he got the more brutal punch.

"It has claimed over forty lives in that section alone. The last time Andrea hiked there, she lost her footing and almost her life because of that worthless... never mind." Donna closed her eyes and waved her two hands before her, trying to erase that memory. "Andrea brushes the incident off, but she could have been another casualty if it wasn't for the kindness of another female hiker that day."

Brent couldn't believe someone else called Knife's Edge the Mountain of Death. Though logically, he knew it was a bit of an exaggeration, as the mountain had claimed less than one hundred lives. "That's an insane idea. Is she looking to die?" This section of the mountain was nothing anyone in a wheelchair could achieve. Brent faced the mountain once a year, every year. Sadly, he knew all too well the lives - four in particular - that the mountain had swallowed, but it wasn't the mountain's fault; it was his. Blaming the mountain for his mistake wasn't right.

"See, it's crazy," Donna said excitedly, raising an octave.

"I'm still not sure what this has to do with us," Brent reflected on the matter at hand.

Donna started talking and didn't stop until they agreed to her plan. "God Bless you both! See you at Guido's in one hour." Brent followed Joe's eyes, glued on Donna, as she sashayed out the door.

What had Brent gotten himself into?

Chapter 3

♥

"**D**ON'T YOU THINK JOE is just the cutest thing ever?" Donna gushed out as she drove Andrea to Guido's.

"I guess if you like the goofy type of guy. I mean, he's attractive enough, but something about him tells me that he could reach that annoying state of goofiness pretty quickly, but I didn't pay too much attention to him."

As much as she told herself not to, Andrea couldn't deny that Brent had rented a lot of space in her head. It's too bad he had to be so strong and smell so good. His woodsy scent kicked her pulse into overdrive. At one point, Andrea thought she'd seen care radiating through his eyes. She wanted to remember him as the mean Grinch who alienated customers. That thought would protect her heart.

He hadn't even flinched when Andrea expressed her frustration with him. He'd told his staff that she was demanding. In fact, he had the nerve to justify himself. "*You are very determined. I didn't want your determination to get you or my staff hurt, so on the contrary, it was very professional.*" Did this man ever quit? He knew it all; he was always right ... and drop-dead gorgeous.

His large hands stuck out to her. The way they felt on her back filled her with warmth. He had to be over six feet tall. Andrea wasn't good at determining people's height anymore. Everyone towered over her in her chair.

Stop that! The most gorgeous man on the outside can lose all his appeal when his insides are like rotten tomatoes. The last thing Andrea wanted was to notice his handsomeness, but it just couldn't be avoided.

"Andrea!" Donna shrieked. "You're not even listening to me." Donna waved her hand in front of Andrea's face.

This whole experience would have been enjoyable if it hadn't been for Brent's bossy, sour attitude, irritating her.

"I still think you should get to know Brent better. I bet he would go on many adventures with you if you let him."

Andrea scoffed. "I wouldn't get too cozy, Mary, matchmaker. You're clearly into Joe, and if you set Brent and me up, I guarantee all those adventures you don't want to do with me, you'll be doing with Joe."

Maybe Donna was right?

Definitely not. Andrea had spent the last year and a half adapting to life by herself. She wouldn't let some overbearing brute come into her life and treat her like a child who needed direction.

"Gosh, I never thought of that." Donna looked concerned, causing a heartfelt laugh to fill the car.

Heavy traffic on the way to Guido's slowed them down. If going to this restaurant hadn't been a tradition for her, she would be at home watching television, relaxing on her couch, and planning her next adventure.

Considering her success today, she wondered if she could climb any part of Mt. Katahdin. The Knife's edge might be a little tricky, but Andrea had never limited herself before being in a chair, so she wouldn't start now.

"I suppose it wouldn't be too bad if Joe asked." Donna winked.

Andrea jerked her head to her left. "Are you kidding me? You'd do something because a man you think is hot asks you, but me, you tell me to fend for myself."

Donna giggled. "That's not what I meant. But you must admit, having a cute guy help you through an adventure is a lot more fun."

Nodding her head, Andrea agreed.

Donna crowed, "Speaking of hot guys..."

Andrea shook her head. "Don't start that again. I can't deny that Brent is good-looking, but we definitely wouldn't work."

Donna pulled up to the curb in front of Guido's. "Why wouldn't it work out?"

A truck, high off the ground, caught Andrea's eye. If she wasn't mistaken, it was the same truck she'd seen at Adventure Park when she'd left. "I know you've been trying to set me up since Kyle ditched me, but I am too independent to date anyone, especially someone like Brent. He argued with me for months about doing the easy zip line course."

Donna shook her head. "Right." She smirked. "I can imagine how difficult it would be to date a super hot guy who's worried about your well-being. Whatever shall you do?"

Donna brought her hand to her chest, pretending to be dis-
traught.

Oddly enough, Andrea's temperature had risen when
Brent held her, but she'd never admit it to Donna, who was
doing everything she could to push her toward him. The
idea of someone like Brent - strong and successful - ever
taking an interest in her was impossible in Andrea's mind.

Finally, they reached Guido's door. As much as Andrea
loved Donna, she couldn't wait to eat and get back home,
where she didn't need to think about Brent or anything else
except her next adventure.

Chapter 4

♥

"MAN, YOU SHOULD HAVE taken a real shower if you were just going to bathe in cologne," Brent teased Joe as he drove them to Guido's Italian restaurant.

Joe punched Brent's right shoulder, but it didn't phase him at all. He laughed at him and gave him a look, asking, *is that all you've got?* "I couldn't shower; I needed to ensure you didn't bail."

"Funny. I shouldn't even be here. The woman can't stand me. Anything I say, she'll do the exact opposite to prove a point. I know her type." Brent shook his head. "This will backfire in Donna's face; mark my words."

Unfazed by Joe's pestering, Brent focused on the road, unwilling to give in and admit that Andrea was easy on the eyes. His friendship with Joe had survived a lot, so Brent knew that Joe was trying to rile him up, to make him spill his thoughts. Truth be told, Joe had always thought he got the best of Brent, but he hadn't. Brent never told anyone, including Joe, anything he didn't want to reveal.

Brent and Joe strolled into Guido's about five minutes before the ladies were expected to arrive. They grabbed a couple of seats at the bar next to two females who fluttered their eyes and smiled. The ladies tried their best to get Brent and Joe's attention. The key word being *tried*. Brent noticed them. It was hard not to when they applied their makeup with a spray gun and forgot most of their outfit at home. He didn't give them a second glance.

"How are you going to pull off Donna's plan?" Joe asked as he took a swig of his drink.

Brent set his drink on the bar slightly harder than he'd meant. Brent reminded Joe that this might have been Donna's plan, but he, Joseph Hudson Hardy, became her number one accomplice, ditching the twenty-year brotherhood they'd built from their first day in Kindergarten. Brent recalled the day when Joe dumped him for Emely, one of three girls in their class, who convinced Joe that he wanted to play on the swings instead of in the sandbox with the Tonka trucks. The man lacked resolve.

Brent knew determination better than anyone. He hadn't been nominated for the USA Today High School Football Player of the Year Award by hesitating to push himself to the limits. Like it was yesterday, Brent remembered Will 'The Pill,' who had torn Brent down daily, telling him he was too small to be a linebacker. Brent lifted weights regularly and pushed himself at practice until he earned the strong-side linebacker position.

Andrea had struck him as determined, too. He'd seen that same intense look in Andrea's eyes. *Trying to change that woman's mind about hiking on Knife's Edge will require something more than spending time with the likes of me.*

Brent's ex-girlfriend had never cared what he said or wanted, so why would some woman who already despised him be any different? Brent thought Donna would need a new plan by the night's end, and he hoped she would count him out.

"Andrea will see right through this. If she wants to kill herself, I'm not going to have any part in it. I can't go through that again." Brent released a big puff of air, deflating his lungs and spirit.

Joe gently tapped him on the back to show his support. "Let it go. It wasn't your fault." The bell above the door chimed, stealing Joe's attention. "Hey, look," he said, pointing toward the door with his thumb. The ladies had just entered, "It's showtime."

Brent's chest cinched tight, his heart pounded like a jackhammer on overdrive. She didn't dress for the restaurant's fancy image. Her seafoam green leggings matched her eyes. The oversized sweatshirt hid her toned upper body. Heat flooded his core and every limb despite the air-conditioned restaurant.

Joe started toward the ladies. When he realized he was alone, he glanced over his shoulder and, through gritted teeth, urged Brent to follow.

Nervously smoothing his hair, Brent trailed behind. Once he stopped in front of Andrea, he still didn't know what to do with his hands, so he smiled and crossed his arms over his chest, which made his muscles bulge. He noticed that the movement caught Andrea's attention. She must have realized she was staring at his muscles. When she quickly lifted her eyes, probably hoping he hadn't witnessed her gawking, Brent smirked as their eyes locked. The faint pink that rose to her cheeks sent an inferno through his stomach. He thought he glimpsed a sparkle in Andrea's eyes but quickly dismissed it, remembering that this was the same woman who had told him off and left him just a few hours ago. Despite their earlier encounter and his discomfort around Donna's plan, he felt an overpowering contentment like he was where he needed to be right now, making his blood surge through his veins. His body temperature rose even more, well beyond a safe level.

"Hey guys," Donna said in a voice too high for this to be a casual run-in. Brent noticed Andrea eyeing Donna suspiciously. "What are you doing here?"

When Joe didn't answer, Brent spoke for him. "We thought we'd get some dinner. How about you ladies?" Brent needed to get control of his eyes. They'd drifted back over every one of Andrea's features. Now she caught him ogling her. The only difference was the reaction. She countered his smirk with a full-blown scowl. *Yup, she hates me.*

"We're here for dinner too. How funny. Should we get a table for four instead of two?" Donna's nervous voice shook. Brent realized this woman should not quit her day job, whatever that was, because she would never make it as an actress. Brent tried to figure out what made her more nervous: Andrea finding out she orchestrated this meeting or Joe's proximity. Brent caught Joe's eyes. He tilted his head slightly, trying to tell his buddy to give the woman some breathing room. Either Brent wasn't good at giving directions, or Joe wasn't good at following them. Donna casually moved to the left a step.

When the hostess approached, Joe pointed toward a table for four. "We've decided to eat together. Can we snag that table there?" The hostess stood erect behind the podium and checked the board before her. She lifted her head, smiling at the couples, agreeing to the change. Allowing Donna to pass, Joe placed his hand on the small of her back as they followed the hostess toward the table. Brent couldn't believe how quickly Joe was moving. He must really like her. "Come on, you two," Joe called over his shoulder to Brent and Andrea, "let's eat. I'm starving."

Brent moved the extra chair away from the table for Andrea. She quietly thanked him, but not before telling him she could have moved it herself.

"Should I put it back so you can?" His tone was more gruff than he intended. She just rolled her eyes and dismissed his question.

"So, Brent," Donna started as she grabbed the last menu off the table, "tell me how you ended up owning the best ropes course in Southern Maine."

Silence.

"After months of listening to you ramble on, I can't believe you're at a loss for words right now." Andrea's slightly curt voice annoyed him.

Not that he owed her an answer, Brent expected she'd bug him until he gave her one. "Well, after my last competition, I used my winnings to purchase Adventure for You from Dave. I renamed it Adventure Park after we added the miniature golf course and go-carts." Brent rubbed the back of his neck as little beads of sweat formed at his hairline.

"Everyone seeking a thrilling experience could have one at our business without traveling to the Andes or the Great Barrier Reef. It's been a great couple of seasons." Brent glared at Joe, warning him not to mention Samantha, the main reason he had purchased the business.

"'*Our business*'? Did someone else purchase the park with you?" Andrea inquired before sipping water through her straw.

Brent gawked at Andrea's lips wrapped around her straw. It wasn't until she scowled at him that Brent ripped his eyes off her. He'd upset her today, and now he was disrupting her evening, too.

Joe came to Brent's rescue almost instantly. "I partnered with Brent shortly after he purchased the park. He couldn't handle all the bookings, hiring, and payroll. You name it, I had to help him with it."

Both girls chuckled.

"Don't get me wrong," Joe continued, "I hate all those aspects too. We need to hire an office manager, so neither of us has to be burdened with the paperwork."

"There you go, Donna. That's right up your alley." Andrea smiled encouragingly. "Donna is an accountant by profession but chose to work in an office because she lacks confidence."

Brent rested his elbows on the table while they chatted. He continuously clenched his biceps and released them. The tension in the air wreaked havoc on his insides.

"Are you a professional athlete or something?" Andrea tried to ask casually, turning her attention back to her menu. Brent liked how cute Andrea looked with flushed cheeks.

"No, I just like to be active," Brent revealed.

"Well, you mentioned a competition. Which one?" Andrea's tone exposed her lack of patience for his vague answers.

Brent felt uncomfortable sharing his physical activities, knowing his presence tonight had one purpose - to convince Andrea she couldn't climb Mount Katahdin. He'd already tried to limit her activities, which hadn't gone well.

"Sorry. It was a duathlon. Nothing big. I mean, I'm not an Olympian or anything." Brent gulped his water to stop himself from saying anything else."

"What's a duathlon?" Donna inquired.

"It starts with a 10K run, a 40K cycle, and it ends with another 5K run," Brent explained.

"That sounds absolutely ... dreadful." Donna scrunched up her nose, and a V formed between her eyebrows. Based on her earlier comment, Brent wasn't surprised by Donna's answer. She wasn't the adventurous type by nature. "As a matter of fact, I don't think I could run that much even if an ax murderer were chasing me."

Andrea tipped her head back and laughed. The sound vibrated through Brent's chest. An insane thought pierced his mind - *take hold of that sweet sound with your lips. Where did that thought come from?* He would never kiss Andrea, not because he didn't find her attractive, but because he did. She'd probably rip his lips off if he ever tried to kiss her.

The waitress had come and gone with a second round of drinks and took everyone's dinner order. Brent had his forearm resting on the table. When Andrea had passed her menu to the waitress, her knuckles had brushed against his arm and sent a jolt of electricity running through it strong enough to startle him. Of course, the jump had caused Joe and Donna to stop dead in their tracks. Flabbergasted, both Andrea and Brent whipped their arms to their respective lap. Brent didn't appreciate the way Joe knowingly smirked at him. Nor did he like that Donna was giving Andrea the same look.

Andrea smiled shyly. "Sorry." She whispered.

"No worries." Brent gazed at Andrea, who was twisting her hair around her finger. He imagined weaving his fingers through her hair and just tasting her lips. With as much fire that came out of her mouth, he figured he should help her extinguish them. Brent pulled at the front of his shirt, allowing air to pass through in an attempt to cool himself. It had been eons since Brent had even thought romantically about a woman, let alone had one raise his irritation level to the boiling point. He wondered if the air conditioner had broken down because he felt on the verge of heat stroke. *This is wild. The woman hates me. I just met her...in person.*

When the waitress delivered the food, Brent silently bowed his head to say grace, placed a napkin on his lap, and started eating. It wasn't until after he swallowed his first bite that he realized she'd been gawking at him.

Why is she staring at me? Brent had apologized for the contact, realizing it bothered - maybe even repulsed - her that he'd accidentally touched her arm.

Donna and Joe used the waitress's presence as a distraction to whisper who knows what to each other. Brent heard the word dating, but that was it. They would be disappointed if they tried to set him and Andrea up. The woman hated him, and the only thing she had going for her was her looks; that's not enough for a relationship.

Brent spied Donna tapping Joe's arm with her hand, pretending he had said something. "That would be a great idea!" Donna's zealous squeal revealed her nerves.

"What?" Andrea inquired, looking up from her plate.

"Joe and Brent climb Mount Katahdin every year, and they are very worried that you may be in over your head trying to accomplish Knife's Edge, so maybe all of us could go rock climbing instead."

Brent squeezed his eyes shut and set his glass down on the table.

"Really? So you guys," Andrea waved her hand back and forth between Joe and Brent, "after meeting me for a hot minute, think you know what I am and am not capable of? Hmm, that's interesting." Andrea's sarcasm was evident. She took a sip of her drink, hopefully to prevent her from saying anything else. When she put her drink down, she looked squarely at Donna, "Lemme guess, you were behind all this.

"Um...I...um..." Donna sputtered.

Brent wished the table could swallow him up and spit him out hundreds of miles away like a tornado would do. He knew this conversation would get messy.

"Donna knows enough to ask for help when she needs it, and she couldn't stop you alone." Brent knew Joe had inserted his foot instantly.

"Is that so?" Andrea slapped her palms on the table. She interlaced her fingers. Brent had used that strategy himself when trying to keep his composure. "So now you've also assessed that I am an idiot - not smart enough to ask for help. Have you ever considered that I don't need anyone's help?"

Joe apologized, but Andrea shrugged it off with her head-strong attitude.

"Andrea, I called the guides in Baxter. They said that under no circumstance should anyone in a wheelchair try climbing Knife's Edge. I mean, who do you think you are, Henry Brownstone?"

"Who?" Andrea questioned.

"I looked it up." Donna shrugged and continued, "He was a professional rock climber. He got into an accident that left him paralyzed from the waist down. Then, after significant practice - eight years after his accident - he completed his first climb in his chair." Donna let out a big sigh. Observers could see how hard it was for her to stand up to her friend.

Andrea's eyes looked troubled. For a moment, she was contemplating what Donna had said. "So you're saying I need to practice more before I attempt to climb?"

Brent stared at her in disbelief. Before speaking, he tried to choose his words carefully. "Have you ever climbed this part of the mountain before?" He already knew the answer but asked anyway.

"As a matter of fact, I have." Andrea emphasized the "t" in *fact,* like that helped her case somehow.

"Have you trained for the climb?

"Of course," Andrea shot back - her voice full of vinegar.

"Have you trained for the climb in your chair?" Brent's forceful tone surprised everyone at the table.

Donna slapped her hand on her forehead. At the same time, Joe placed a hand on her shoulder to comfort her.

"How did your first climb of Knife's Edge go? Brent regained his composure.

"I'm here, aren't I?" Andrea responded grudgingly, avoiding his question.

"The fact remains," Brent slightly mocked Andrea, "you aren't here in the same way you were when you climbed. The state you're in now does not bode well for a climb like this."

"If it hadn't been for that hiker who saved you when you lost your footing on that narrow passage, you wouldn't be here." Donna snitched.

Narrowing his eyes at Andrea, Brent challenged her. "You can withhold all the information you want from me; you don't owe me anything, but like with the zip-lining, I am just trying to keep you safe."

Closing her eyes, Andrea sighed. "I can still see the young hiker. The ends of her dark black hair in a high ponytail rested on the top of her hiker's backpack. Her long, lean leg muscles were in a squat position, and her toned arms extended out with her hands like vice grips around my wrists. She pulled me up, landing in a heap, pinning down her legs for a brief moment." No one at the table said a word. "I only have a selfie to remember her."

"She'd run off after saving Andrea to meet up with the rest of her party." Donna continued the story. "Andrea developed that picture and hung it in her hallway to remember the hiker daily." Andrea opened her eyes but continued staring at the food she had barely touched on her plate. The emotion in Andrea's voice had Brent seeing this woman differently.

Brent couldn't be sure, but it looked like Andrea had doubts about climbing. Hopefully, Andrea would realize she wouldn't be able to wheel herself up the mountain, and even if she could, it would be too dangerous. "I greatly appreciate all of your concerns, but only I can decide what is best for me."

Maybe he changed his opinion too quickly. "If you want to kill yourself, I can't stop you," Brent murmured.

Andrea gasped. "No one asked you to."

Brent stuffed his face with a bite of braciole without responding.

The rest of the meal was uneventful, mainly since Andrea hadn't engaged in the conversation. He couldn't believe he'd thought for a brief second that she had a heart or, at the very least, seemed human.

Andrea pulled her wallet out to pay her portion of the bill. Brent held up his hand. "I've got it."

"No, thanks, I've got it." She dropped her cash on the table.

"My goodness, Woman, give a man a break," Brent growled, but Andrea had already rolled away, leaving him talking to the air.

They met with Joe and Donna, who were waiting at the door. Brent was ready to get home, watch the rest of the game, and forget about everything to do with Andrea.

"Hey, Buddy! Joe's upbeat tone set off suspicious alarms in Brent's head. "I want to take Donna to the pond in Pullman Park for a walk.

Brent's head dropped, knowing a ruse when he heard one. He turned to Andrea, who'd already started to protest. "Donna, I would have driven myself if I knew you weren't going to bring me home."

Driven herself? Brent hadn't even thought of Andrea driving herself around.

"I'm sorry, Andrea. I'm sure Brent wouldn't mind dropping you off. Right, Brent?" Donna smiled.

He clenched his jaw muscles and released quickly - a tell-tale sign of frustration. The idea of having Andrea in his truck sent his stomach into a high-speed roller coaster. When he'd spied Joe's face, he knew that Joe and his new attraction had set him up. That annoyed him. Unfortunately for him, it also stoked the simmered fire he'd felt earlier. He silently nodded to show his willingness.

Andrea silently agreed, too. Donna kissed her friend on the cheek and rushed out the door with Joe. "I'll call you later."

Brent held the door for Andrea as they exited the restaurant. "I'm parked up the hill a bit. Do you want to wait here? I'll go get the truck?"

"Do I look like I can't get myself up the hill?" Andrea blasted back.

"Nope," Brent used a curt tone to respond. "I was just trying to be nice. I'll do my best to ensure it doesn't happen again."

Once they reached his truck, Andrea said, "I can get home on my own. There's no way I'll get in there," she pointed to the high off-the-ground truck. "Even if I weren't in this chair and used the curb, watching me get into that beast would still be a funny show."

Brent's mouth twitched. Calling his truck a beast brought out his manliness. "You're right; you probably wouldn't get up on your own. I don't imagine you would ask for my help, either."

Andrea's eyes burned into his skin, clearly contemplating what she should do. Without a word, Andrea started to wheel away. Brent hopped in front of her, placing both hands on her chair's arms. He leaned about six inches from her face. "Is it just me, or do you refuse help from everyone?" The sound of his voice was direct.

"I am very independent."

"Everyone needs help sometimes, so you clearly dislike me for whatever reason. But my mother raised a gentleman, and I won't let you change that. Just let me bring you home, and you never have to see me again."

"Promise?"

"Funny." He didn't mean it literally. Isn't that just something people say to get others to do whatever they requested?"

Andrea had hesitated so long to answer Brent didn't think she would. Finally, she nodded her head in agreement. "Okay. Thank you."

Brent slowly pushed her chair toward his truck in a strange but neutral silence. Brent set the brakes on Andrea's chair before he opened the truck door. As he lifted her, a strong whiff of her cottony, beachy scent filled his entire body.

"Brent!" He turned and locked eyes with... *her.*

No, No, No! I thought she moved.

Panicking, Brent completely lost his mind. He quickly pressed his lips on Andrea's and held them there, stiff, for a moment. Fireworks exploded in his chest. That's when he relaxed and deepened the kiss, hoping she'd kiss him back and not make him look like a fool in front of *her*...again. When he heard a soft moan escape from Andrea, he parted his lips to deepen the kiss even more. Unable to breathe any longer, Brent pulled away, waiting for Andrea to open her eyes. Once she did, Brent sent her a look with his eyes that he hoped said sorry, thank you, and wow all in one. Gently, Brent placed her on the passenger side of his truck and avoided answering her silent question, which he already knew was *what the heck?* He was relieved that she didn't smack him.

Out of the corner of his eye, he detected that his unpleasant surprise still lingered. Brent folded Andrea's chair, placed it in the bed of his truck, and quickly threw a hand up to acknowledge the woman before hopping in the driver's side.

Andrea's scent had already filled his truck, and his jelly-like legs weren't helping him make a quick getaway. The engine roared to life. Brent pressed down on the seat with his hands while he adjusted his body. He fastened his seatbelt, ripped the engine into gear, and bolted away. Brent tapped the gas a little too aggressively, and Andrea's body banged back against the seat.

"Sorry." Brent couldn't manage any other words at that moment.

"Who was that back there?" She asked, her eyes full of compassion.

Brent struggled with his inner self: *drive faster to get this woman out of my truck, or go slower and soak up her delicious scent.* He couldn't remember a time - ever - when a girl; no, she wasn't a girl, she was all woman - challenged him this much, causing him to harbor so many ambivalent feelings.

"She is a cross between Lady Tremaine and Cruella DeVille." Brent gripped the steering wheel, not wanting to get into this conversation.

A burst of unexpected laughter gushed from her mouth before she could whip her hand over her lips. "I'm sorry. I didn't expect you to be funny. You've made me laugh twice now."

"Hmmm. That's okay. I never expected you to laugh, so we're even." Brent's teasing tone made Andrea smile again.

His foot let up on the accelerator. All on its own, his body had decided to extend the drive. The silent tension present a few moments ago disappeared with her angelic laugh. Brent's mind returned to that kiss. For a surprised woman, she was a great kisser. He'd taken note of her soft, full lips that tasted like watermelon.

Instead of getting to know her better, he'd daydreamed of that kiss and what one might be like if she'd been expecting it. He needed to be a gentleman and not fixate on kissing her again. Heck, he'd be lucky to see her again.

Once he arrived at Andrea's ranch-style home, he jumped out of the truck after he slammed it into gear. Brent took a deep breath. The hot, muggy August weather did nothing to cool him down. The easy part was pulling Andrea's chair from the truck bed and positioning it near the opened passenger side door.

Thinking about holding her again was the challenge. "Is it okay to pick you up again, or should I just see if you can slide out?" Brent sported a half grin to let her know that he was joking. Bantering with her brought him joy. It was even better when he glimpsed a slight twinge of her upper lip. *Success!*

"Well, if you're going to have all those muscles, you might as well put them to work. No point in me doing it all."

Brent froze. *Where did that come from? Was she flirting with me?*

Then, she changed the subject. "It's obvious you kissed me to make that woman jealous; you could at least tell me the story."

Man, she's direct. When Brent placed his arm under her legs and the other arm around her waist, she naturally positioned her arm around his neck. With their faces inches apart, heat burned in his belly. His eyes met hers. Those emeralds captivated him. His chest coiled like a snake getting ready to attack. His heart thumped against his ribs. Brent hungered to feel her lips again. Did she feel this, too?

Trying to be a better gentleman than he was moments ago when he assaulted her lips on the sidewalk, Brent settled Andrea in her chair before walking her to the door. She tried to rush inside after she unlocked her door, but he grabbed her arm. Her eyes shifted between his and the hand on her soft skin, making his body thrum like rain hitting the window. Brent straightened his spine and stuffed his hands in his pockets. "Look, I'm sorry I ticked you off ... a lot today. It's just... I... well... I want you to know I'm truly sorry."

"I'm sorry I was so rough on you, too. It's hard to go from climbing mountains, snorkeling, surfing, biking, kayaking, hiking, skiing, snowmobiling, and everything else I did all by myself to needing help or not being able to do them at all, like climbing."

Brent breathed in a silent relief that, in Andrea's own way, she just admitted that everyone was right tonight; she was not ready for that mountain. Brent wondered if she'd end up going rock climbing. He should invite Andrea to go with him. Brent hadn't considered going on a date in years, which scared the daylights out of him. His hands, tucked securely in his pockets, began to sweat even more.

"Am I dreaming? Did you apologize to me?" Brent dramatically pressed a hand to his chest.

"Don't make a big deal about it, or I'll take it back." Andrea's stern voice and teasing eyes captivated Brent's attention, making his heart thump a little harder.

"No can do, Woman. Unless I get amnesia, I won't ever forget that apology." Brent lowered this body, balancing on the balls of his feet. "Seriously though, I can only imagine how I'd act in your situation, so I forgive you."

"Thank you. Donna's the greatest best friend, but she's not an outdoorsy person. There isn't anyone who tries harder than her, hence today's adventure."

"There must be someone who you can still enjoy life with?" Brent shocked himself with that question.

"If that's your way of asking if I have a boyfriend, no, I don't. Not anymore." Andrea twitched her lips slightly, "Although, some would think you were my boyfriend the way you kissed me back there."

Brent felt his cheeks grow hot. He didn't rush to explain anything, so Andrea queried. "A girl who's been pestering you for a date, and you wanted to make her think you were taken? How close am I?"

Brent let out a big belly laugh, "Hardly. She was someone I thought I knew, but she turned out to be the complete opposite."

"I imagine. If she's comparable to women who abuse children and kill puppies, she must be one evil person. How do you know about Disney villains?"

Brent smiled. "My sister was big into the movies when we were younger."

"Phew, I thought you were harboring away in your house watching Disney movies every night after work."

Serious as stone, Brent returned the banter. "I can't handle Disney every night. Once a week on a Saturday night is my preference."

Their laughter sounded like sweet music. It went together like peanut butter and jelly. That is the one thing from his childhood that he still enjoyed.

Ask her about rock climbing!

The silence inched just beyond awkward. "Thank you for the ride, Brent. Goodnight."

"Goodnight, Andrea." She gently shut the door, leaving Brent still standing there.

Brent tried to gather his thoughts on the way home. Andrea had seemed to ease up after that kiss. However, Brent couldn't imagine the kiss had anything to do with it. Maybe she just started to realize that her friend, Donna, cared about her and didn't want her dying on a mountain; just thinking those words stabbed daggers into Brent's heart. While he didn't want to see anything happen to Andrea, the culprit of the current pain spurred from the last family hike on Knife's Edge. He was glad he hadn't asked Andrea out. Brent could never let another person get close to him. Regardless of how beautiful Andrea was, he needed to keep his distance to protect both of them from broken hearts or possibly even death.

Brent arrived home fifteen minutes later to find Joe sitting on his couch. Without a doubt, Joe had been waiting for him to return so he could capture the details of his evening after dinner. If he hadn't ditched him, he'd know. Brent wasn't in the mood to share the latter part of his evening, not even with Joe. "What are you doing here?"

Joe ignored Brent's question. "How'd your evening go?" Joe's sing-song voice annoyed Brent. "Donna said that she'd never seen Andrea so flustered before. Andrea is attracted to you, Man, and that's why she's so gruff."

"I doubt that." A slight spark of interest swirled in Brent's chest as he remembered his stolen kiss. Andrea did appear less grumpy after this. Maybe there was some truth to Joe's statement.

"What took you so long to take Andrea home? I've been here for at least twenty minutes."

Brent casually responded, unwilling to tell him about the kiss, "Everything takes time." Brent shut the door, figuring his friend wouldn't leave any time soon.

"Did you kiss her?" Joe propped himself up on the couch.

Brent moved around the room, picking up loose items as he started rambling about how ridiculous Joe was even to suggest that. Since Brent refused to ask Andrea for an actual date, he would probably never see her again. He reminded

Joe that, as his best friend, he knew why Brent couldn't get involved with her or any other woman. ... ever.

Joe waved his hand, dismissing Brent's negative, self-blaming thoughts. "You kissed her, and you like her!" Joe blurted out, interrupting Brent's chatter.

Brent approached the couch, grabbed Joe's arm, and guided him to the door. "I am happy with my life the way it is. I cannot let some beautiful brunette mess with my head. I've been through enough, and I thought you, of all people, would understand and back off."

Once Brent positioned Joe at the threshold, he continued, "If you like Donna, go for it, but as for Andrea and me, there's nothing there." With that, he shut the door in his best friend's face.

Joe yelled through the door, "Next time, wipe her lip gloss off your lips before you try to convince anyone of how you feel! Sleep tight, Buddy Boy!"

Brent wiped his lips with the back of his hand. Two things became crystal clear to Brent: one, he wouldn't sleep much, and two, he would never forget that kiss!

A NDREA DIDN'T MOVE FOR what seemed like forever. Bruno, her German Shepherd service dog she adopted nine months ago, rushed over to her when she shut the door and rested his chin on her lap. She gently stroked his fur to calm her nerves and process her thoughts. Andrea finally wheeled herself to the bathroom attached to her bedroom and washed up for bed.

After changing into her pajamas, she hoisted herself into bed. She slammed her head against her pillow, recalling the roller coaster ride of emotions that had hurled throughout her body that evening. The unreasonable dictator she'd fought for months to use his zip lines turned out to be a terribly attractive man. Bruno took his place on his doggy mattress right next to the bed.

Andrea knew Donna was behind the meet-up this evening. She would call her first thing in the morning ... for sure! Giddiness and frustration filled her entire body. Why was this man having such an effect on her? Her brain hurt thinking about this. No man, not even her ex, Kyle, had affected her like this. But Brent stirred something inside

Andrea that she couldn't quite explain and wasn't sure she liked the state of her mind.

Tears seeped out of the corners of Andrea's eyes, falling flat to her pillow. "Mom, I need you here to talk with. You always knew the right thing to say." Andrea's voice fell to a whisper, "I miss you." Bruno trotted over, his nails clicking on the hardwood. He rested his snout on the mattress. He always knew when Andrea needed fur time. She found the most peace while stroking above Bruno's eyes to the base of his neck. Between the tears and petting, Andrea drifted off to sleep.

Bright and early, Andrea's always–set alarm sounded, jolting her from a deep sleep. She embraced the foreign feeling invading her body - like a teenager with a crush. Not that she had one. Yeah, Brent was attractive, and she loved the sweet way he blushed last night. She sighed. But, it'd been a long time, since before her accident, that a man had impacted her the way Brent had. If she were being honest, she wouldn't have minded another kiss, yet that hadn't hap-pened, nor did she expect it to again. He'd only kissed her to make that woman jealous. The fizzling embers holding firm in her stomach left her queasy.

This was the same man who tried to prevent her from zip-lining. He was able to do any adventure he desired. Brent wouldn't want her dead weight to lug around ... lit-erally.

She heard Bruno stir and head out of the room. Moments later, the slap of the rubber doggy door let her know he'd be back after taking care of business. Now, she had her own business with Donna to settle. A few taps on her phone later, Andrea heard ringing. She didn't mind that it would wake Donna, given that Donna's meddling led one hundred percent to the anguish gripping Andrea's mind, body, and soul.

When Donna answered in a groggy whisper, Andrea started in, "How was your evening with Joe?" Andrea didn't wait for her to answer; she continued spewing comments that she knew would get Donna to feel guilty and admit her part in the plan, "I thought you were my friend? Trying to push Brent and me together doesn't seem very friendly."

Donna took a deep breath. "Good morning to you, Sunshine."

"Funny. Donna, what were you thinking?"

"Look, I saw how you two stared at each other. There was something there, am I right?"

Andrea didn't argue with her friend. She recalled the puzzling electricity that ran through her when they briefly touched. Nothing compared to the cascade of lightning bolts that flooded her body when he kissed her.

But it was to make someone jealous; it was not like the kiss actually meant anything to him. Besides her physical reactions, Andrea wasn't sure if the kiss meant anything to her. Andrea had to figure out how to forget the kiss that had set her on fire! Being that close to Brent and listening to his deep, husky voice had made it hard for Andrea to be annoyed with him.

"Look, Andie..." Donna's nickname for Andrea cut right to her. She started calling her that after the accident when she wanted Andrea to listen to her. Andrea knew Donna didn't use it casually, so whatever she had to say, Donna meant it with all her heart. "You deserve to be happy; if you never try, you never will be."

Andrea considered what her friend said for a moment. "I am happy," she pushed out, even though she knew she sounded a little strained. When he returned to the room, Bruno must have even heard the stress in her voice, too. He rested his chin on the mattress, and Andrea slowly petted Bruno's head.

"No, you're not truly happy. You've adjusted to life ... somewhat. I've never been as outdoorsy as you. I'll keep trying, but you need someone who loves it as much as you do."

"I thought I had that." Andrea waited momentarily and added, "I know you never liked Kyle."

"Nope. I knew he was a sleazeball. I'm just sorry you had to find out the way you did."

Donna had questioned Andrea many times about whether or not she loved Kyle. It wasn't until recently, when her friend had said, "*I notice you're spending more time grieving the idea of being left and not as much time grieving the man that left.*" that Andrea questioned it herself.

After last night's kiss, Andrea was totally over Kyle. Realizing hindsight is twenty-twenty, Andrea had never experienced fireworks like she did last night. Heck, even a slow-burning flame for Kyle might prove she had built some feelings for him, but she came up with nothing - no past feelings, no current feelings, just emptiness. She had loved the adventures they went on, but that wasn't enough for either of them. She hated running into him. He always looked so happy with his new girl, and there Andrea sat in a wheelchair.

"Andrea, are you there?" she heard compassion in Donna's voice.

"Yeah," she sighed.

"What's on your mind?" Donna questioned cautiously.

"I'm sorry, Donna. I know my life is missing adventure, and I am a little down."

"I don't believe your life is missing adventure. You just completed the ropes course, and you completed and won your first wheelchair race a few months ago. I think you're fixated on the things you can't do, even if it's subconscious and..." Andrea waited for Donna to finish. "you're missing someone to love and share these experiences with." Donna paused again for a moment. "Don't get upset, but I haven't heard you thank God for anything in a long time. You used to thank him for the simplest things, and now nothing."

Andrea's chest tightened. "I've lost everything - my parents, my legs, and my boyfriend - not much of a loss, I know, but still."

"Think of everything you have, Andrea. You have me; that should be enough for anyone." Her teasing tone lifted one corner of Andrea's mouth. "I know you've never cared about money, but you got enough for the rest of your life. You had a custom house built—"

"—I had to. Without major renovations, I couldn't live in my parents' house anymore." *Why was Donna giving me a hard time about this? Hadn't I lost enough already?*

Donna sighed. "I didn't mean to upset you. The old Andrea would have said, 'God may have taken my ability to walk, but he gave me what I need to live my life in a chair.'"

Silence.

"What are you doing?" Andrea asked when Donna sounded a hundred miles away.

"Checking a text, I just got from Joe."

Andrea thought the two of them were cute together. She hoped he would be good to Donna.

What?!" Donna screeched.

"Is everything okay?" Andrea's voice, etched with concern.

"Oh no, you don't pretend nothing happened. I can't believe you didn't tell me you kissed Brent."

Darn. She didn't want to have this conversation so early in the morning.

"Spill it," Donna demanded.

Andrea validated that a kiss did indeed happen; however, it didn't mean anything to him because he just wanted to make some girl jealous.

"Pshaw. Tell yourself whatever you need to get through the day, but I saw chemistry in the making at dinner last night. Maybe the kiss started as a decoy, but this could be the beginning of something special. "I've got to go, Andrea. I'll talk to you later, bye."

Pulling her phone away from her ear, she saw her phone's wallpaper and wondered why Donna had hung up so quickly. That could only mean one thing: more meddling.

Urg!

Andrea plopped herself in her chair, jolting the memory of how gently Brent had placed her down in his truck and then her chair - she longed for that again. Andrea's saddened heart sent her conflicting messages. Either she wanted to avoid this man or be near him, but both these emotions bouncing back and forth like an Olympic ping pong ball match had taken their toll. She felt more exhausted now than she had last night.

Andrea wondered if Brent would even want to see her again. He didn't mention the kiss; she had to, so obviously, it hadn't meant anything ... to him. What did it mean to her?

The extra wide entryways with pocket doors and hardwood flooring in all the rooms except the bathrooms and kitchen, which were porcelain, made maneuvering through her house smooth. Rolling to her bathroom counter, which sat about six inches lower than a standard setup, Andrea stared at herself in the mirror that hung directly above the space. Andrea's eyes pierced with tears, unable to recognize the person she'd become. Donna may be right - Andrea was different now.

That Bible verse about reading the Word but not following it was like looking in the mirror and not recognizing the person staring back. Andrea sadly realized this was her. She needed to focus on what she had accomplished and what she could complete in the chair. Finding someone to share it with might be more of a challenge. Donna had turned into Benedict Arnold, so Bruno was all she had left.

Washing her face and brushing her teeth revitalized her spirit just as much as it did her body. Andrea's emotions were playing tug of war with her mind. She wanted to do things herself, but in the case of climbing The Knife's Edge, she really couldn't ... not yet. Also, she couldn't dismiss the electric shock that ran through her body every single time it had been in contact with Brent's yesterday. *Urg! Stop thinking like that. A man like him would never look at you as anything but a burden.*

A chime from her phone pulled Andrea from her thoughts. She snatched her phone from her bed to see who texted. The unfamiliar number caused her to toss it back on the bed to finish getting ready. Autumn was her favorite season, though throwing on shorts this time of year was definitely easier. Andrea grabbed her phone and headed to the kitchen for breakfast.

In the spirit of trying to look for the positive, Andrea admired her kitchen for a few moments. It was built with her in mind. She could reach everything she needed without too much effort. She placed two hard-boiled eggs, some almonds, and a banana on the table. Andrea filled her bottle with ice water and rolled to the table when her cell phone alerted her of an incoming text - the same number as before. When she pulled up her texting app, she stared at her phone screen as if she'd looked at Medusa. There were two messages from Brent.

347-904-7389

Hey, this is Brent. I got your number through Donna and Joe. I just wanted to make sure you weren't too sore from yesterday. I hope you had a great time.

Hey, it's Brent again. Donna just left the park and asked me to let you know that she's on her way to your house.

Finally, a man texts me to see if I am okay. Why did it have to be the jerk who didn't think I could handle adventures and used me to make another woman jealous?

Andrea's thoughts flashed back to their sidewalk kiss. She could still feel his hot breath beating against her cheek. The heart-stopping, mind-blowing, I'm going to crush you kiss had lingered in her stomach. It hadn't been until he kissed her that she noticed his deep, husky voice, which gave her heart palpitations all night.

Who was that girl from last night? Andrea had the urge to thank her. If she hadn't shown up, Brent never would have kissed her. That kiss set off rockets in her body. Unfortunately, now she knew what she'd been missing. Finding a man who could be interested in her and kiss like Brent would be challenging.

Andrea typed and erased three times before sending off her text.

Andrea

Thanks for the heads up about Donna. I'm no more sore than when I push myself around daily.

As she reread the text, it didn't sound as friendly as it could have. So she sent another one with a smiley face.

Andrea

Thanks for making it happen.

Three dots appeared on the screen before she could set her phone down. She felt absolutely ridiculous - like a silly schoolgirl enamored with the popular boy - butterflies fluttered in her stomach. Thank goodness she hadn't eaten anything yet.

Brent

I'm happy we could make things work.

She waited for more dots. Nothing. With each passing minute, her stomach sank even more. Her belly hollowed out. Imagine a butterfly catcher appearing, and like a thief in the night, he stole all their goodness away. She set her phone down. She told herself to be relieved. Andrea didn't need any complications in her life, and Brent was a big stumbling block.

Chapter 6

♥

IF THERE WAS ONE thing he could do well, Brent was able to alienate women or let them down. First Samantha, and by golly, he'd done it again with Andrea. It'd been almost a week since Brent had texted her. Instead of taking his time to think, he pushed out, *'I'm happy we could make things work.'* Of course, she hadn't responded. He hadn't given her anything to respond to.

Despite Donna and Joe's constant pestering, he hadn't tried to contact her ... at all. What reason did he have to contact her? She despised him. Instead, he'd laid in bed every night since, thinking of that kiss. The woman had fire in her veins. Her feistiness reminded him of Samantha. He knew how that ended, so every time Andrea entered his mind, Brent shook it away. It was for her own good. He convinced himself that he didn't mind her fire. Perhaps it had to do with her transformation to a civil human being by the time he'd dropped her off that night.

But now he dragged himself around work, unable to focus. He'd never felt this way about a woman before, and her unwelcome intrusion irritated him. He had no ill feelings toward her when he thought about it. Yes, he thought she was difficult, but he never had any distaste for her like she did him.

"Are you going to store those harnesses or just carry them around the store all day?" Joe broke into Brent's thoughts.

Looking down at his hands, he shook his head before trudging to the wall and hung them on the appropriate pegs.

"Distracted much?" Joe chuckled.

Brent flashed Joe a fake smile. "Shut it."

"Let's suppose you do what Donna and I suggest, and you ask Andrea out. What's the worst that could happen?" He followed Brent back to the office.

Before he could answer, Joe's phone alerted him of a text. Without question, it was Donna. They had been texting nonstop today. He was happy for his friend; he really was. But why did they have to push him with Andrea? Brent had thought he truly loved a woman once before. Cherie loved to be outdoors. They went biking and hiking all the time. Brent got her bungee jump and snorkel. The day they were scheduled to skydive, she arrived at his house and dropped a bombshell on him. Their relationship. It had all been a sham. Cherie didn't like him. She'd been using him to get back at her ex-boyfriend, who now wanted her back. The kiss he shared with Andrea hadn't been far from his mind, but now he felt guilt. He kissed her to make Cherie jealous. Couldn't that be overlooked since he enjoyed it so much?

He might have fallen hard for Cherie had it lasted longer than three weeks. A few months after that hard news to swallow, he had taken the life of the best woman he'd ever known besides his mom. From that point on, he vowed never to get close to any woman, knowing she'd probably break his heart, and if she hadn't, he'd probably kill her, unintentionally, of course. Andrea had already lost so much physically he'd be evil to take anything else from her, especially her life.

Joe let out a big belly laugh, catching Brent's attention from his desk. Alright, maybe he wasn't thrilled about his friend's happiness. Today, Joe hadn't let a minute go by without talking about Donna or Andrea. Brent had never seen his friend get this sucked in so quickly. He must really like her, or they both want the same thing so badly they teamed up to make his life difficult.

Exhaustion overwhelmed Brent. He needed to get out of there, but three orders still needed his attention. When Joe's laugh radiated throughout his office again, Brent growled, "Are we really out of souvenir shot glasses?"

Shoving his phone in his pocket, Joe stopped in the doorway. "Yes, we are, Grumpy. You know, if you did something other than hide in your house or work, you'd be more pleasant. Just an idea, you could take Andrea on a date."

"Well, thank you, Suzy Sunshine." Brent tapped a few keys on the computer to fulfill the order.

"Wow, you really do have it bad. If I say her name, are you going to combust?" Joe cackled like the Wicked Witch of the West.

Maybe it's time to get a new friend. "I'll be just fine." Brent stood and grabbed his coat.

"Are you leaving to see Andrea?" Joe smirked.

Brent's death stare was enough for Joe to put his hands up in surrender and step out of the threshold. "I'm going to check on Steve. He's the lock-up ropes supervisor today since Dylan called out. Some of us have to work around here."

"Hey, I'm working," Joe yelled at Brent's back.

"On getting a date, maybe," Brent shot back before the front door slammed shut.

The late summer, early autumn weather in New England was so tricky. Yesterday, it had been seventy-two degrees; today, it was forty-nine. To us, New Englanders, forty-nine was still warm when thinking about the cold months ahead beckoning us, but after a day like yesterday, it dropped Brent's spirit a little more.

Though he'd spend the winter skiing, snowshoeing, climbing, snowboarding, and any other activity that suited him, he hated closing the business down for the season. He needed to come up with a plan to stay open year-round.

Without warning, Andrea popped into his thoughts. He'd never tell her this, but he did feel bad that her life was tipped upside down. He couldn't imagine what he'd do or how he'd feel in her situation. If he had to guess, he'd be one angry dude.

It took about thirty minutes for him and Steve to close up for the night. "Thanks, Boss, for the hand. I would have been here another thirty or forty minutes if I had done this alone."

"No problem. The fresh air helped me more than I helped you. Trust me." He moved a chair - the one they put in place for Andrea - to the other side of the building.

"Everything okay?"

Brent wouldn't tell his employee that his chest ached whenever he thought about never seeing Andrea again. Nor would he share that he felt guilty for kissing her to make Cherie jealous. He didn't expect to see his ex and couldn't let Cherie think for a second that he was alone. Now, all he could think of was Andrea.

"It must be something good. I've never seen you smile like that."

"What? I wasn't smiling."

"Oh, okay, Boss." Steve's knowing eyes flanked him.

"You look like you're good here. Thanks for all your hard work today. See ya tomorrow." Brent escaped toward the main building.

He wasn't surprised that his face had beamed like the sun; he'd been thinking of Andrea. Anytime she appeared in his mind, so did that kiss, which sent rockets off inside Brent's chest, and the blaze that ignited last night continued to burn in Brent's gut. After walking Andrea to her door, he vowed to stay away from her so that, in time, the fire she set ablaze would be extinguished.

After a miserable week, since he'd sent her a dumb text and was harassed by Joe, Brent decided he should wear a "Caution: Extremely flammable" sign. He knew that one spark, one little twinkle of Andrea's eyes, and Brent's body would erupt into an uncontainable inferno. He rapidly pulled back and forth at the collar of his shirt to let air flow. He didn't even know this woman. These feelings were ridiculous.

Back in the main building, Brent invited Joe for pizza and playing cards.

Joe had different ideas. "How about you join Donna and me at Freddy's tonight - all appetizers are half off until eight."

"Not tonight. I don't feel like being set up again." Brent didn't want Joe to think he was naive for even one moment; he knew it was a plan to bring Andrea and him together again.

"Come on, Bro! It's time you move on." Cherie was just a stepping stone, and Samantha wasn't your fault.

Brent stormed to the back wall without saying a word. He didn't want to talk about either Cherie or the accident. "Just drop it!"

Brent organized and hung up the harnesses the camp director had dropped off before gathering all his campers onto the bus. He recalled the kids who soared the lines today. Brent enjoyed the visits from campers. It reminded him of his summers with his sister. Four years his junior, she always wanted to do everything he did. He recalled her gleeful smile when their parents had finally let her zip line on her fourth birthday. It only took one run for her to love the activity. Once they saw her passion for any activity, their parents let her try almost everything. On her sixteenth birthday, Brent took her skydiving. She loved it so much that she begged Brent to go again three months later for his birthday and take her. He smiled, recalling his sister's exuberant personality. Brent used to go skydiving often. He hadn't been since that last time with his sister. That would have been his reintroduction into the sport if Cherie hadn't canceled.

"Does your cheery mood have anything to do with that kiss?" Joe asked, smirking and pulling Brent back to the present. When he didn't confirm or deny his friend's suspicions, he declared, "You don't have to admit it; I have other sources."

Andrea must have told Donna. Was she mad that I kissed her, or...did she like it? Nah. "Lemme guess Donna told you? Brent inquired.

"No, you just did!" Joe laughed, crossing his arms. "That never gets old. How can you always fall for that?" Joe walked behind the counter to help hang the last few harnesses and to get the details. "Oh, and by the way, I told Donna this morning." He shrugged his shoulders. "The lip gloss gave it away."

Great. Now Andrea will think he's talking about her. That'll give her another reason to hate me.

Hanging the last harness on the wall a little too forcefully, Brent finally explained what happened with a sigh. Brent admitted that the kiss meant something, or he wouldn't be so distracted and grumpy, but Brent had refused to incriminate himself further. He stormed into his office and shut the door to place his last order so he could go home.

Why was this woman affecting him so much? He didn't need to complicate his life. He had the business and his adventures; that was enough for him. Brent couldn't deny the chemistry between him and Andrea, but he also knew the woman wasn't his biggest fan either.

Thirty minutes later, he got a text from the two overnight security guards confirming that the park was secure. Brent and Joe locked up the store and parted ways, vowing to see each other bright and early the next day. Joe had tried one last time to get Brent to change his mind about joining him and Donna, but he refused.

Getting in his truck, Brent noticed that before Joe had even put his seat belt on, he pulled out his phone. He'd texted with or talked to Donna all day. He thought Joe was acting like a teenager. Brent was happy for the guy, but he might be a tad jealous, too, if he was being honest. Why couldn't he move on? Refusing to date the last few years seemed silly when Joe gave him a hard time about it, but he couldn't get his mind or heart to let go of the hurt, the pain, and the guilt. Most of his guilt of late was his distance from his Creator. Too much pain and death drew him away.

Brent's parents asked him frequently to start back up at church. He hadn't. He didn't understand how they could move. As he sighed, feeling disappointed in himself, Brent pressed the push-start button on his truck, and it roared to life.

His mind drifted back to Andrea. It was easy to be annoyed with the woman when she gave him a hard time on the phone. But seeing her in person was altogether different. Her sad eyes told him enough. Andrea was bitter and upset, probably about being in the chair. He saw her beauty, too, and not just the physical. When Donna came barreling down the zip line like a banshee, Andrea's smile reached her beautiful green eyes.

He let out an exaggerated breath before pushing the voice activation button. "Call Joe."

Joe picked before the second ring had time to finish. Without a sweet beginning filler, Joe blurted out, "You need to ask Andrea out."

"Would you stop?" Brent moaned. "Do you want to watch the game tonight?"

"Yup. I'll be over with pizza." Joe hung up before Brent could respond. He ran his hand down his face, wondering if asking Joe to come over had been a mistake. His friend's suspicious eagerness troubled Brent the entire way home.

From an early age, Brent's mom had taught him a lot about reading people and being observant. She'd always complained about his dad not noticing her facial expressions or tone to understand her moods. His mom had claimed she was doing 'Brent's future wife a big favor' by training him early on. Little did she know, she'd wasted her time - finding a wife wasn't in his life plan anymore.

Joe barreled through his door, pulling Brent from his thoughts. "Pizza's here." The man's happiness filled the previously gloomy room.

Brent grabbed the roll of paper towels from the counter and two cokes from the refrigerator. After setting them on the table, he noticed Joe's nervous expression. "What?"

"Maybe we should use plates instead."

"Why?"

Joe wouldn't make eye contact with Brent. "What's going on?"

The doorbell chimed before Joe could even acknowledge Brent's question.

"Joe?" His voice box clogged, preventing him from saying more. The Joker–sized grin on Joe's face let Brent know who was behind the door.

To calm his nerves, Brent ran his fingers through his hair and straightened a couch pillow on his way to answer the door. He couldn't believe that Joe would do this to him when they were supposed to watch the game together. The Boston Bullets were his favorite basketball team. He never missed a game, apparently, until tonight.

With his hand on the doorknob, he hesitated. For the first time in a very long time, he prayed silently. *Lord, please forgive me for turning away. Please watch out for Andrea. Don't let me hurt her. Help her not hate me.*

Brent felt instantly lighter in spirit. He couldn't be mad at his best friend for trying to make him happy. Looking back at Joe, he stated dryly, "Give me more of a warning next time."

Chapter 7

♥

"Apartment 2C." Donna had a skip to her step and a twinkle in her eye as she pressed the elevator button. The elevator was surprisingly fast for an older building.

Reaching the apartment, Donna knocked. The sound matched the smile plastered on her cheery face. Even though Donna had refused to tell Andrea where they were headed, she imagined Joe whipping open the door to embrace Donna, knowing her best friend wouldn't be this excited to see anyone else.

To her surprise, when the door finally opened, Brent stood frozen at the threshold, his smile surprised like he hadn't been expecting the ladies this evening. He locked eyes with Andrea. The smile that reached his eyes now let Andrea know he was okay with her being at his place. Andrea stayed focused on his lips a little too long. Then she noticed that his Adam's apple moved up and down slowly before he said, "Come in," and moved to the side. Andrea followed Donna.

Once inside, Andrea's traitorous eyes trailed from Brent's slightly messed up hair to his fitted short-sleeved shirt that showcased the muscles in his arms and onto his gray athletic shorts, the elastic band resting flat against his rippled abs. Andrea placed her hand on her renegade stomach to hopefully subdue the bounce party taking place.

Unlike Donna, who quickly eliminated all space between her and Joe, who stood in the kitchen, Andrea hadn't moved past the couch, which sat about five feet from the doorway. She felt out of place like she shouldn't be there. Joe and Donna enjoyed spending time together. Brent and Joe were friends. She didn't fit into any of those equations.

From behind, Brent knelt close to Andrea's ear and whispered, "How've you been?" His presence startled her. If that wasn't bad enough, he placed his hand on her shoulder. "Sorry." That sent a wire of electricity through her arm, putting Doc Brown's clock tower experiment in Back to the Future to shame. Based on his smirk, she wondered if he did it on purpose.

He's not supposed to be friendly or show interest in how I am. This is bothersome. He should be as gruff as he was the last few months. "I've been good, how about you?" Andrea clasped her fingers together and squeezed until they were white. From a distance, she spied Joe and Donna watching them.

"She hasn't been good, but she'd never tell you that." Donna shot out. Andrea gave her a death glare. Donna shrugged her shoulders and turned back to her conversation with Joe. It obviously didn't bother her.

Brent sat on the side arm of the couch. He finally wiped the smirk from his face and answered, "I'm a good listener if you want to share anything."

"I'm good. Thanks."

Perfect, me too."

Joe hollered from his spot in the kitchen. "That's a lie too!"

Hmm. What could make his life not be 'good'? He owns the best theme park in the state. He has all of his limbs. He can do any sport he wants.

Brent just chuckled and shrugged his shoulders. "Pizza arrived just before you ladies did. Ready to eat?" The guys had already put the pizza and plates on the table, so only drinks were needed, "What can I get you?"

"Water, please." She wondered how long this awkward evening would last. She should have driven herself. *Definitely.*

When Andrea had first arrived, she'd been ready to un-friend Donna. How could she deceive her? As Andrea nibbled at her pizza, she listened to the trio at the table converse. Joe and Brent shared a story of their most recent scuba diving quest while Donna held onto every one of Joe's words.

"Must be nice." She muttered under her breath.

"What is your problem?" Brent's curt tone grabbed Andrea's attention. She wasn't supposed to notice anything pleasant about the man sitting so close to her; their knees brushed each other under the table. Yet, she caught sight of the inch of stubble on his face that hadn't been there before. It made him look more mature and attractive.

Andrea pulled her bottom lip into her mouth using her teeth, hoping to prevent an outburst.

He cleared his throat. "I can make you something different if you're not a pizza fan." Brent offered. She liked how he attempted to redeem his harsh tone. He chose to focus on her lack of eating and not her grumbling.

Brent's Adam apple moved as he cleared his throat. It looked very kissable. *No, no, no. My mind should not be focusing on his body parts.* Kyle's throat was scrawny, and Andrea hadn't ever noticed that he had an Adam's apple. The comparison between the men surprised Andrea.

"Thank you, that is very thoughtful, but I'm just not that hungry. It doesn't have anything to do with the food." She got lost in her thoughts once more.

How could someone so difficult be so thoughtful? Kyle had always given her a hard time when she didn't eat what he ate. Why was she comparing the two men? Brent would never be anything to her, and Kyle was her ex. Neither had any right to be in her thoughts.

She fibbed. She'd always loved pizza before becoming a hostage to her wheelchair. Fear that she'd be too heavy for someone to lift if necessary overwhelmed her, so she avoided rich foods except after strenuous activity.

Obviously, that fear didn't apply to Brent. When he reached for another slice of pizza and pulled back, his stout muscles shifted, revealing their impressiveness. She peeled her eyes off his arms. Across the table, Donna cleared her throat, gaining Andrea's attention. Her friend's knowing look didn't bother her; she'd already admitted that she found him attractive. Who wouldn't? This would be the time to thank God for not taking her eyesight away.

"Are you too cold?" His attention to the growing goose-bumps on Andrea's arms made her feel even more self-conscious.

"A little." She reluctantly accepted the sweatshirt he handed her. After pulling it over her head, she closed her eyes and sniffed it as she wrapped her arms around her waist. *Wow. he smells great."* She had to reign in her rogue thoughts once again.

Opening her eyes, Brent was staring at her. Undoubtedly, he'd seen her sniff his sweatshirt. *How embarrassing.*

Andrea wanted to roll under a boulder and hide, so a blatant subject change was in order. "Um...so, how was business today?" She took another nibble of her pizza to prevent her from saying anything else.

Brent laughed. "If Joe did anything for the business today, that would have been helpful. I was swamped with orders and cleaned up while Joe dreamed about Donna."

"Aw!" Donna slowly dipped her chin down.

Andrea scoffed. "You expect us to believe that you let Joe get away with that?" Andrea challenged him with her eyes. "You don't let anyone do anything you don't approve of."

"You're going to hold that over my head for the rest of my life, aren't you?"

Andrea narrowed her eyes at him. "Only when it's applicable."

Brent shook his head and rolled his eyes. *What?!* She thought only girls rolled their eyes. Something she'd never admit was how good he looked doing it.

"I was trying to keep you safe." Brent defended himself.

Andrea held her arms wide. "You did a great job. I'm still here." light laughter permeated the room.

They finished dinner and cleaned up quickly. Then, Joe claimed the remote and searched for movies. *Now, a movie?* Andrea wished she drove herself.

Brent had taken a spot on the couch next to Andrea, and fireworks exploded in her chest at his nearness. Brent was an unwelcome distraction. At least she wouldn't have to talk or listen to any of his amazing adventures if we watched a movie.

"*When Harry Met Sally,*" Donna started to call out some of her favorite movies as Joe scrolled.

In unison, the other three declared, "No!"

"*Jerry Maguire,*" Donna held her hand up, pleading.

"Your Tom Cruise crush will have to wait; there will be no *Jerry Maguire* tonight. You better be careful, Joe. Don't take any trips to Hollywood. We'll surely lose her if she even gets a tip of where Tom Cruise might be." Andrea always picked on her friend about her Hollywood crushes.

"Well, at least, I don't love—"

"Fine, Fine, Fine!" Andrea interrupted, "Watch whatever."

"I think I might want to hear this." Brent shifted toward Andrea, smiling. His arm slid down her shoulders, and his other hand poked her in the side."

"Seriously?" Andrea questioned straight-faced. "I can't feel anything below the waist; you think I can feel that?" Brent's face dropped, and he started to apologize before he noticed the corner of her lip move up a little.

"Don't listen to her," Donna flicked her hand toward Brent, "she just isn't ticklish, and I mean at all."

"That sounds like a challenge." Brent's eyebrows shot up quickly and dropped just as fast.

He was so close Andrea could see that the blacks of his eyes had eaten away at the milk chocolatey brown she'd seen before. "Suit yourself." Andrea opened her arms wide.

"Oh no, when you least expect it." Brent's promise implied further get-togethers. That excited and terrified her, especially when he scooted even closer.

"As long as you know, jumpiness and being ticklish are very different.

"I got it," Donna hopped in her seat, "*The Bounty Hunter.*"

"Oh, Gerald Butler. I like him, but I'd rather watch something from his Fallen series. London is my favorite," Andrea offered her suggestion.

"Nope. It's rom-com night," Donna kept scrolling, "and I'm not picking *New in Town,* so just forget it, Andrea."

"You're quiet over there. Do you have any suggestions?" Andrea tried to engage Joe in the conversation.

"Nope. I'm learning so much about you two. This is fun to watch." Joe looked at his friend, "Wouldn't you agree, Brent?"

"Definitely." Brent stretched out his arm on the back of the couch and scooted even closer, closing the gap between their shoulders.

"Is that okay?"

Unable to speak, Andrea just shook her head.

Brent and Joe walked the ladies to Donna's car almost three hours later. Brent took Andrea's chair. Instead of wrestling with it in the trunk, he folded it and slid it into the backseat. Resting one forearm on the car's roof and the other on the top of the open door, he leaned closer toward Andrea. "Thank you for coming over. I didn't care for *The Proposal,* but the night wasn't all bad."

"Oh, I was wondering why you were single, but now I know," Andrea said dryly, pulling her eyes off him and staring out the windshield.

"What do you mean?" Brent challenged.

Andrea turned her head. "'*The night wasn't all bad.'* I feel special; thanks. And what do you mean you '*didn't care for The Proposal'?* What do you have against Ryan Reynolds?"

"He is it, isn't he?" A coy smile filled Brent's face.

Andrea's puzzled look must have been written all over her face since Brent elaborated. "He's your Hollywood crush."

Andrea let out a boisterous laugh. "Nope. Good try, though. What's your problem with Ryan Reynolds?

"Nothing. I like Deadpool. I'm not a rom-com movie man."

"Shocker." Sarcasm oozed from her response.

Just then. Andrea realized she still had his sweatshirt. She leaned forward and pulled one arm from the sweatshirt. "Sorry, I got—"

"—It's okay." Brent held his palm straight at her, signaling for her to stop.

"Thanks for letting me wear this home. I'll get it back to you soon."

"I'm counting on that."

Her stomach dropped, and she silently pleaded for it to settle down. *Did he mean to say that?* She never planned on dating anyone again, even if they were heart-stoppingly gorgeous, like the man currently leaning in front of her, who looked like he had fallen off a magazine cover. It should be illegal to look so good with little effort. Her traitorous body was mesmerized with him.

Fortunately, Donna hopped in the driver's seat, ready to take her home. "Thanks again."

"Night." Brent shut her door.

As Donna backed out of the parking spot, she asked Andrea, "Did you have a good night?

Andrea was quiet for a moment. "I really did. Not that it matters."

Putting her turn signal on, Donna slowed, waiting for a car to pass by before she made her turn. "Why doesn't it matter?"

Andrea scoffed. "We live in different worlds. He lives among the walking. He can still go bungee jumping, climbing, surfing, or whatever he wants to do. I refuse to be a burden on him or anyone else for that matter."

"Do you want to know what I think?"

"Not really. You should stick to driving me home." Andrea smirked.

"I think you like him, and you're afraid."

Andrea snapped her head toward her friend. "Am not."

"Whoa, that was way too quick. You only indicated you weren't afraid. You do like him." Donna bounced in her seat.

Without committing to an answer, Andrea stated dryly. "Yeah, I guess I don't despise him anymore."

Chapter 8

♥

THE BELL OVER THE shop door alerted Brent that he was no longer alone. Looking at his watch, he questioned who it could be since Joe had never arrived before seven fifteen and was only five past seven. Stepping out of his office, Brent froze.

"Hi, Brent." A meek voice that didn't match the viper on the inside prevented him from moving.

"What are you doing here, Cherie?" Brent hoped his cold tone and stiff shoulders sent the message he intended - Go away!

"Please don't be mad at me."

"I'm not mad at you. I don't like people who use other people. It's mean and heartless, and I have no use for them."

"I'm sorry." Cherie stepped toward Brent but froze when he raised his hand, keeping her at bay.

"You already said that when you walked away, I don't need to hear it again."

Cherie sighed. "Yeah, the other night, you made it clear that you've moved on. She's beautiful."

It took a second, but Brent realized she was referring to Andrea. "Yeah, she's beautiful on the inside and out," Brent recalled the wonderful evening he'd had with Andrea last night, but he certainly wouldn't admit anything to Cherie. There's nothing fake about her."

"Brent, I wasn't being fake. I—"

"—I don't want to hash this out again. It's not important to me." Brent gathered the harnesses he needed for the preschool group scheduled for today. "I already wished you well with your boyfriend; there isn't any reason for you to be here now."

"Well, as you know, I do the special interviews for WSXT. They want me to interview you. Your business and your renovations will be the main discussion." She put the fake nail on her pointer finger between her teeth, looking nervous.

"What aren't you telling me?"

Cherie pursed her lips into a thin line and nodded her head. "I might have told the producers that your girlfriend or fiancé is in a wheelchair, and they wanted to capitalize on that story too. They thought maybe she could give hope to others in the same situation; if they saw how she overcame her disability, then they could, too.

"I am not interested in working with you." Brent ignored everything else she said.

"Brent. She's got a story that others should hear. Don't punish the world because you're mad at me."

Bile rose in his throat. "Leave my girlfriend alone."

Joe froze just inside the door. Brent began to sweat.

As Cherie turned to leave, she almost ran square into Joe, who still hadn't moved. "This conversation isn't over, Brent."

"What was that about?" Joe pointed his thumb over his shoulder at the door that Cherie had exited moments ago.

When Brent ignored him and walked off, Joe rushed before him, stopping him in his tracks. "You called Andrea your girlfriend. What did I miss?"

"Nothing." Brent walked around Joe, swiped the papers off the glass top, and rushed into his office. "It was a slip of the tongue, that's all. I didn't want that piranha bothering Andrea."

Joe smirked. "If I were a woman, I'd be all over you. Look at you being protective."

Brent returned to the office door. "Not a word of this to anyone."

Joe held up three fingers like he'd been in the Boy Scouts but hadn't. "I promise." The smirk on his face told Brent otherwise.

Relentless, Joe entered and asked, "Wanna go rock climbing tonight?

Leaving his office, Brent pulled the harnesses from the wall for the first camp group scheduled to arrive at eight-thirty. He couldn't believe he'd called Andrea his girlfriend. Even more surprising, he hadn't minded how it sounded coming from his lips.

She hadn't shown enough interest in him to warrant pretending she was his girlfriend. Whatever. Cherie had surprised him, and it slipped from his mouth. He didn't plan to see Andrea again, so no one would know about this unless Joe blabbed. "Sure, you know I love that?"

"Great! Our reservation is at six-thirty tonight." When Brent shot him a *what the heck* look, Joe smiled and reported,

"Andrea already told Donna she'd love to, so we booked it yesterday."

Duped again! How did they get Andrea to agree to this? "Not a word of my slip to anyone."

The day swallowed Brent up between the paperwork, harness fittings, and safety talks. He had little downtime to fret over seeing Andrea later that evening. But now that he and Joe had helped the last two customers of the night into harnesses, he looked at his watch - five o'clock. Brent ran his hand through his hair to calm his nerves. In an hour and a half, Andrea would be invading not only his mind but also his space. Though a welcomed thought and desire, fear washed over him. Should he tell her that he called her his girlfriend?

By the time the last couple completed their designated course, Brent had realized how late it was. "Joe, I'll have to go climbing another time."

"What? No." Joe moved to Brent's side. "You leave now. I'll take care of locking up and get the all-clear from security. Donna's place is on the way to the gym, so I'll pick her up and meet you there."

Brent agreed. He grabbed his keys and headed for the door.

It'd taken him almost an hour to drive home and get ready. As he threw his gear bag on the passenger seat of his truck, his phone rang. It took three full rings to fish it out of his pocket. "What's up, Joe?" The clock on his truck dash screamed at him to move faster.

"Can you swing by Andrea's and pick her up?" He explained that he had just made it to Donna's and meeting at the climbing facility would be quicker. Since Brent had to go by Andrea's anyway, it made sense that he should pick her up; at least, that's the argument Joe used.

When Brent arrived at Andrea's, he ran his hand through his hair before he knocked on the door. Nerves ate his stomach like it was their last meal.

Andrea opened the door and seemed just as surprised to see Brent as he had been to pick her up. "Where's Donna? I thought she was coming to get me."

"I was closer. I hope that's not a problem." Brent sounded so unsure of himself.

Bruno barked at Brent. It wasn't an *I'm going to eat you for dinner* type of bark, but his fangs alerted Brent. Andrea rubbed Bruno's head. "Shh. It's okay. He's a good one." Their eyes locked briefly before she flicked off the main light, turned on the porch light, and shut the door. "It's fine. If I had known you'd be with us tonight, I could have had your sweatshirt ready."

"That's not a problem. Are you ready?"

"Yup. Let's go." He felt her response throughout his entire body.

Brent searched his brain for something to say after he settled Andrea in the truck. He felt beads of sweat forming just underneath his hairline. Her words: '*he's a good one,*' ran through his mind, clogging any other coherent thoughts from forming. At this point, anything he said would probably come out wrong or stupid, but he had to start with something.

"So Gerald Butler, huh?"

"Excuse me?" Andrea turned her head toward him, but he didn't take his eyes off the road.

"He's your Hollywood crush." Brent's statement was more like a question.

Andrea giggled, "No, though he has the potential for that whole Florence Nightingale syndrome."

He knew confusion filled his face, so he appreciated her elaboration. "You know - man saves woman; woman falls madly in love with the hero who saved her."

"Oh, so it's a good thing when someone saves another person from danger?"

Andrea nodded. "Of course. The majority of romance movies bank their success on that theme.

"So if Gerald Butler told you not to climb the Knife's Edge, saving you from death, would you fall madly in love with him?"

Andrea laughed. "Well, since I don't know Gerald Butler and don't need saving, the likelihood of falling for him is slim to none."

"In all seriousness, I'm glad you realized that the Knife's Edge was something you probably couldn't do right now."

Brent sent Andrea a quick wink. *Did I just wink at her? Where did that come from?* "But just so you know, if I have to get a Gerald Butler mask made up and rehash this conversation, I will do that just to keep you safe."

Andrea dipped her head toward the truck floor. Her flushed cheeks had his stomach doing flip-flops. The silence in the truck hadn't bothered him as much as the guilt weighing heavily on his chest. He may just be kidding about the whole Gerald Butler mask, but he hadn't been able to save Samantha, so what made him so confident that he'd be able to save Andrea in her wheelchair if anything happened to her?

"So, if it's not Gerald Butler, who then?" Brent hoped his persistence paid off.

"Wouldn't you like to know," she flirted.

Yes, I would. "I'll get it out of you soon enough."

After a few beats of silence, he pulled into the parking lot, ready to rock climb. Brent came clean. "I have to tell you something, and I don't want you to get mad. You could say it was a pure accident, a Freudian slip." He shifted his body toward Andrea and saw that he had her full attention.

"That woman we saw on the sidewalk after Guido's..." Just mentioning the situation brought him to the kiss, and his chest constricted. He wondered if Andrea thought the same since a light pink hue formed on her high cheekbones. "She came into the store today, and in the heat of the moment, I referred to you as my girlfriend."

Crickets. She just stared at Brent for a moment before acknowledging what he said. "That's it? I'm not, so it's no big deal. Thanks for telling me, though."

He half expected her to get all dramatic like she had when booking the zip-lining, but she hadn't. If Brent read it correctly, her calmness equated to a lack of interest. He felt the disappointment throughout his body, like a slumped-over Charlie Brown with a rain cloud over his head.

Brent opened Andrea's door, placed her chair next to the truck, and started to pick her up. "Does transporting me classify as you saving me because I'd hate for there to be any confusion," She returned to their teasing state.

"Do you want it to classify?" Brent unexpectedly flirted, not sure why. Maybe it came from his internal war of wanting another kiss but repeatedly convincing himself that another kiss would be detrimental to his well-being. Now Andrea had confirmed that she was not interested in him.

His comment left her speechless for a second before she found her voice. "I guess we'll have to see."

Andrea placed her palm on Brent's chest. Big mistake. His pulse quickened beyond his control.

"Back up, I can get this," Andrea said with a playful but insistent voice. Brent backed up, letting Andrea reach for the inside of the door to support herself. Everything was going fine until Donna distracted her.

"Andrea!" Donna yelled across the parking lot as she and Joe walked toward Brent's truck. When Andrea looked toward her friend, she missed the door and headed for the hard, unforgiving blacktop that awaited her. Fortunately, Brent swooped in and wrapped his arms around her arms and chest like a big bear hug. He held her just long enough to take in the unmistakable ocean, cottony aroma oozing off her skin.

He placed her in her chair. "Are you alright," Brent asked a little husky.

"I'm fine now, thanks to you. I guess this one is classified as a save." Andrea couldn't pull her eyes off the short stubble that gently scraped against her cheek moments ago.

Brent grabbed his gear bag from the back seat before shutting the door. As he flung the bag over his shoulder, he stared directly into Andrea's eyes with a hint of romantic gesture, "Looks like I'm your Gerald Butler." He strutted away like he one-upped her.

Andrea rolled her eyes, "Would you stop it? You're not even close." She rolled just behind him, trying to catch up.

"Until you tell me who your Hollywood crush is, it will be Butler." Brent didn't give her the satisfaction of turning around; he just spoke loud enough so she could hear. The thought of Andrea falling for him because he saved her warmed him to the core. *Holding Andrea again had felt heavenly.*

Forget her Hollywood crush. Brent longed to be Andrea's crush.

Chapter 9

♥

BRENT, JOE, AND DONNA put their harness on inside the gym while the staff helped Andrea into hers. "Focus on your harness, man; Andrea will be all set," Joe teased Brent, who couldn't take his eyes off Andrea. Donna tried to stifle her laugh but couldn't.

Brent looped the safety strip down the middle loop, hooked the clip, and twisted the metal security piece … tight. He secured the next safety strap and hook, then dropped his hands, "See, I'm focused."

"You're not fooling anyone!" Joe finished tightening his and Donna's harnesses and walked toward the staff so they could check his handy work.

"Is this your first time climbing, Donna?" Brent knew she didn't prefer athletic movement.

Donna shook her head. "No, this is one activity I like, but in a gym. Not on a mountain where a slip means death, not just a broken arm."

"Are you okay?" Donna placed her hand on his forearm. "Joe, is he okay? What did I say?"

Brent's stomach dropped. His head spun. Fortunately, he hadn't eaten lately, or it would appear again. He had tunnel vision, and his breathing started to become shallow. Joe directed Brent to inhale slowly and let it out through his mouth. Brent repeated the process, trying to steady his breathing. Anxiety. He knew the problem; now, he just had to overcome it. Closing her eyes, Brent repeated his breathing three more times, and he had calmed himself enough to begin.

His anxiety attacks were getting shorter, thankful. "Sorry. My thoughts got away from me."

"No, I'm sorry. I didn't mean to upset you." Donna's compassion was evident.

Once the staff checked the trio's harnesses, they started climbing. The employee with Andrea had her watch a safety video before allowing her to begin. Brent was glad the video convinced her to stay in her chair to scale the wall. He'd always been told that was the more productive climbing method. He silently prayed for her, knowing that it wouldn't be easy regardless of which strategy she chose and she may not make it to the top the first time.

"Way to go, Donna!" Brent heard Andrea yell as Donna scurried up the wall faster than a Floridian lizard spooked by a tourist. Even Joe wasn't as fast as Donna, though Brent knew his friend was letting her reach the top first.

He felt eyes watching him as he started his climb. Turning his head, he spied Andrea at the wall farthest away, studying him. His heartbeat sped up as she watched him navigate the wall with as much ease and grace as he could reign in.

"Miss, excuse me. Miss, are you ready?" A staff member, whose name tag identified him as Dan, tapped Andrea on the shoulder. "We're ready for you."

The wall called her name. She was ready for this. Andrea used her forearms to hoist herself up on the lowest jug. Dan started shouting out directives. Do this without stopping. Swing right to grab the yellow mini jug and then quickly swing left to grab the blue jug.

She tried to block out everything except for Dan. After about two minutes, she completed the beginner wall. Her friends had already maneuvered through the three beginner walls and were starting the more advanced levels that used different, more challenging holds and grew in height about two feet. She knew Donna would become more athletic if given the right incentive. Thank you, Joe.

Andrea was now straight across from Donna at the base of the intermediate wall. "Nice work, Andrea! I bet you'll perfect this too so that you can enter the Paraclimbing Olympics, right?" Donna joked.

Andrea didn't enjoy this as much as mountain climbing, but the idea of competing sparked her interest. "That's a great idea; I must look into that!" Andrea could tell by the look on Donna's face that she was kidding, but why not? *I am just as capable as anyone else.*

"Ready?" Dan got her all strapped in and checked its se-cureness. About halfway up, Andrea's triceps burned. *It wasn't a 'my arms are burning, so I'm going to give in be-cause I'm tired.' Andrea's arms were almost as numb as her legs.* Dan must have seen it because he asked her multiple times if she needed to be done. Andrea refused.

"Large swing to the blue jug. Come on, Andrea, you can do it," Dan encouraged. Weight on the left, swing to the right quickly." Dan hollered the final directions in quick succession, which Andrea appreciated.

Her friends shouted their encouraging words in between Dan's calls. After three more swings, Andrea rang the bell at the top of the wall. The sound of the bell filled Andrea with a sense of accomplishment.

Once on the ground, Dan unstrapped her chair. Donna hugged her. "I'm so proud of you."

"Thanks. It was all God. My arms were going to give out." Andrea let out a breath.

Donna smiled. "That's my girl. You are so right."

"How do you feel?" Brent asked. She melted as she locked eyes with him, his face beaming. At that moment, she ad-mitted to herself that she'd reached the smitten stage, which petrified her.

She'd watched Brent use every one of his limbs - some-thing she could not do. *How could he ever be interested in me?* "I feel great. Exhausted, but great, ya know?"

"I get it." Brent smiled.

Taking control of her flip-flopping stomach, she caught Dan before he walked away. "Thank you for the great directions. I couldn't have done it without your support."

"Anytime. It's fun to work with people who don't give up easily." Dan grabbed the strap off the ground. "Have a nice night." he waved to the four of them as he retreated.

About that time, Joe and Donna were wishing Brent and Andrea adieu. "Bye, guys. This was a blast. We'll have to do it again." Donna cheerfully waved her hand toward the should-be couple when she and Joe were three steps from the door.

"Wait a minute," Andrea's urgent tone was ever-present. "That's it? We're not hanging out more?"

With a grin, Joe piped up, "Brent, you'll hang out and make sure Andrea gets home safely, right?"

Brent cast a look in Andrea's direction. She tried to gauge his reaction but couldn't. "Yeah, of course." When he smiled, Andrea's heart fluttered ever so lightly.

"See ya." Joe and Donna waved as they bolted from the building.

"You killed those walls in there." Brent encouraged Andrea as they made their way to his truck.

"Thanks, but I think you killed a few more than I did." Andrea hasn't been able to accept a compliment since the accident. Admittedly, Brent's sounded authentic to her, like he genuinely meant it, yet she still struggled.

As they reached the passenger side door, Andrea smirked at Brent. "You didn't overexert those muscles of yours, did you? I don't want to end up on the ground." *Why am I flirting with him? My poor heart is going to shatter. I can see it already.*

Brent chortled. "As I recall, you almost ended up on the ground before you climbed, so I think I'd take a chance on me if I were you."

Andrea couldn't help but laugh. He pretended that she was slipping out of his arms. She clung tighter to his neck. Her inability to breathe through her laughter lit up her heart like fireworks on a dark summer night. This man was getting to her. He wasn't the pigheaded, unbearable man she'd spoken to on the phone. Brent was someone she wanted to know and spend time with.

"I've got you, don't worry." He smiled inches from her face. Andrea noticed a small dimple form at the side of his mouth. Andrea rested her palm against his chest. His heart was racing just as fast as hers. The kiss she had been reliving and wishing for since their night at Guido's would finally happen again. The tip of Brent's tongue gently wet his lips. Andrea could barely contain herself. She inched closer to him. Then, just like that, he tenderly placed her on the seat of his truck. "See, I told you I was the right man for the job." She felt his warm breath on her cheek, making every nerve ending that still worked tingle.

Andrea could have sworn she saw him smirk as he rounded the front of the truck. She couldn't determine if his slight breathlessness was a physical excursion or interest. His eyes bore into hers with what seemed like genuine interest, but what did she know? She'd stayed with Kyle longer than she should have. Kyle had never been one to show affection. She recalled the first time they'd gone climbing, and he helped her with the harness. He'd worked hard not to touch her during that process. He didn't brush his fingers on her leg or waist, nothing. Maybe it was her imagination, but she could have sworn that Brent ran his thumb gently over her arm when he lifted her tonight. *Stop comparing them. One was your boyfriend, and the other only used you to make someone else jealous...not once but twice.*

She hadn't thought too much about him calling her his girlfriend since he first told her, and butterflies erupted from the hallows of her stomach. She believed him when he said it was an accident. Of course, it was. She was dead weight, literally, to everyone around her, especially a man like Brent. She wished her feelings would get with the program and realize that, though. The more time her mind focused on him, the more she imagined herself hanging out with him and Bruno if they could warm up to each other.

"Would you like to get something to eat, or do you want me to take you home?" Brent briskly rubbed his palms together, pulling Andrea from her thoughts.

"Sure, let's eat. You decide where." Andrea ordered, her tone playful.

When they arrived at Guido's twenty minutes later, Andrea chuckled. "Seriously? You're not sick of this place?"

"It was the only place I knew you liked, so... here we are." He hopped out of the truck before she could respond.

Aw! That's so thoughtful. Andrea couldn't remember when Kyle had done anything to make her happy. With everything, he'd had an underlying purpose or goal that would make him happy. Andrea shook her thoughts of 'ol *what's his face* and focused on the broad-shouldered hunk pulling her chair from the truck bed. She was treading down a dangerous road. Nothing good could come from allowing her feelings to reign freely.

"Your chariot awaits, milady." Brent used an awful seventeen-hundred French accent that made her giggle.

When he lifted her this time, his arms were a warm blanket blocking the cool, almost autumn air from piercing her skin. The instant he set her in her chair, a chill blasted her, causing her to shiver. He grabbed an extra chamois shirt from the back. "Sorry, this is all I have." He held it open for Andrea to slip her first arm through and then the next.

"Thank you. This is perfect." It was, too. She didn't know what he wore for cologne, but it smelled woodsy with a hint of vanilla. She still hadn't returned his sweatshirt and didn't plan to until the scent wore off.

Brent got them a quaint table in the back of the restaurant. "Is it okay if I move the chair for you, or would you rather I let you suffer?" His lip turned up at one corner. Andrea recalled her not-so-nice response during their last visit.

"I don't mind moving it myself, but I wonder what all these people would say if you stood idly by and let me suffer with the chair," Andrea smirked, waiting for his comeback that never came.

He leaned close to her ear, and she felt his warm breath on her cheek. "I hope you know I'd never let you suffer with anything."

Oh, Dear God, help me. Heat rose up her neck and settled in her cheeks.

Andrea couldn't remember a time when she'd laughed so much. An hour and a half had flown by. As they shared a brownie sundae for dessert, Brent dabbled his finger in whipped cream and wiped it on her cheek.

"Aw." Andrea grabbed her napkin to clean it off, but Brent gently grabbed her wrist, suspending it mid–air.

"I'd hate to waste that. He kissed her cheek, letting the sugary topping fill his lips. When he pulled back, he had a little left on his upper lip that he promptly licked off.

Andrea's breath hitched. *Breathe, girl, breathe.* This couldn't be the same man who made it difficult for her to zip line.

"Would you like anything else?" Brent asked.

She shook her head as she swallowed the mouthful of water - a little oasis for her dry mouth.

During the car ride home, Andrea had recovered from the surprise whipped cream kiss and engaged in small talk. It appeared that Brent was forcing himself to keep his eyes on the road. His firm grip on the steering wheel mimicked the knots in the pit of her stomach.

He nearly drove off the side of the road laughing when she declared that Steve Urkel was her Hollywood crush and tried talking like him. "I used to be able to do the Urkel dance. Now that I'm in this chair, the world doesn't know what it's missing. I could have gone all the way on Dancing with the Stars with that move."

"You lie!" Brent roared. "Do you mean the character or the actual actor? Never mind, don't answer. I know you're lying."

"Yeah, I am, but I love that show. As a matter of fact, I love all the old sitcoms. People today have to keep redoing old movies and television shows because they aren't creative enough to think of their own."

"Now that I believe." Brent pulled into her driveway. "You don't have to tell me your crush, but it will come out someday."

After getting Andrea situated in her chair, they strolled to the door together. "I had a great time, and I'd like to get together after Joe and I return from our trip to Mount Washington."

"When are you coming back?" Andrea could hear the disappointment in her voice. She hoped Brent hadn't.

"It's just a weekend. I'll be back on Monday."

Andrea's smile dropped. "I can't."

"No worries. I thought we'd moved past our initial issues, but that's okay." Brent released his hands from his pockets. "I'll see ya around, Andrea."

"Wait." Andrea reached for his arm; her hand warmed instantly. He stopped. "You don't understand." She quickly explained herself. "I'd like to go back out with you, but I can't on Monday. I am seeing a doctor about an experimental therapy program that may help me walk again."

"Seriously?" Brent faced her, lowering to the balls of his feet. "Is it dangerous?"

"Everything comes with risks." Andrea deadpanned. She could tell he was trying to find a way to respond. "They said I would be drained initially, so I didn't want you to think I changed my mind or anything if I was too exhausted to go out."

"Thank you. Is it okay if I call you when I get back?"

"Sure, that would be nice." Andrea found herself leaning closer, and so was Brent. She'd been waiting for another kiss since that first night outside Guido's.

Brent gently pressed his lips to her cheek, the one that missed out on the whipped cream. He lingered there a half a second and pulled back. When Andrea slowly opened her eyes, his whole face smiled at her. Heat rose into her neck.

"Goodnight, Andrea."

She watched Brent start to walk away. Then he turned around. "You need to go in the house before I leave. I'd walk you in, but Bruno seems a bit protective, and I'd like to keep my limbs and clothing in one piece."

"He's not that bad." She rolled her eyes.

As she wheeled toward the door, she heard him yell, "Of course, he's not that bad if you're the one he's protecting."

Andrea wheeled herself to the other side of the door, turned, giving him a quick wave and friendly smile, then shut the door and locked it.

His truck came to life moments later, just like Andrea's heart had earlier that evening. There is no denying her attraction to Brent. She wondered if the feelings were one-sided.

Chapter 10

♥

Brent's shoulders were relaxed and his spirit free, like he had been talking to an old friend. Regret tugged at his heart when he pulled out of Andrea's driveway. Brent didn't want the night to end.

Knowing he would see her again had his heart leaping. His desire to kiss her when he transported her to her chair almost overwhelmed him, but he controlled himself, not wanting to push her too quickly. His heart had nearly dropped when the awkward silence waiting for Andrea to explain why she couldn't see him had settled like a dense fog.

"What was I thinking?" He ranted aloud as he drove down the street after dropping Andrea off. "She wanted me to give her a real kiss. I saw it and did nothing." He slammed his hand against the steering wheel hard enough to get his frustration out.

There wasn't any point in getting upset. He and Joe were leaving for New Hampshire in the morning, and he wouldn't see her for a few days. He needed to focus on getting a good night's sleep to be safe climbing.

The next day, Brent stared at the trail he and Joe were about to tackle. Trepidation ran through him. "This is going to be easy compared to dealing with Andrea."

Joe chortled. "For as long as I can remember, you've said, "The best things in life are worth hard work," have you not?"

He nodded. It never impressed him when others used his advice against him. "Let's go."

"Give me a second." Joe pulled out his phone and tapped the speakerphone. "Hey, Donna. How's everything going?"

"It's going great," Donna reported cheerfully. "you left seriously detailed notes. I'd have to be an idiot to mess up, and I am not, so we're great."

"That's Brent, Mr. Details." Joe teased. "I'll see you in a couple of days. Thank you for helping us out."

"Any time." Donna hesitated.

"Is there something you're not telling me?" Joe asked cautiously, grabbing Brent's attention.

"Well," Donna started and then stopped.

"Just spit it out, Woman."

"Steve, I think he's the ropes supervisor. I had to let him know we were dating..." Her words dropped off, and all Brent could do was laugh.

Joe backhanded him in the chest. "Ow."

"You let Steve know we'll have a sit-down Monday morning."

Donna chuckled. "Oh, okay. Bye, Joe."

Joe zipped up his side pocket after securing his phone.

Mount Washington is known as the *Most Dangerous Small Mountain in the World.* It is undoubtedly Brent and Joe's most challenging climb in a while. They return at least once a season to endure a few trudges up the mountain. They started in shorts at the bottom and were forced to slip into pants and a winter jacket at the summit.

Usually, on their climbs, they focus on them and the mountain. Today, Brent struggled with thoughts of Andrea all day. Every time Joe opened his mouth, he spoke of Donna. Standing on the summit, looking into the vast open space below, Brent did something he hadn't done in a while. He prayed. He'd lost his way with God after dealing with his and Cherie's breakup. While he continued to give thanks for his food and instinctively said, *Thank God* or *Thank you, Jesus,* he'd never reconnected with God after the accident.

Lord, I am so sorry for deserting you. I am still mad at you for taking Samantha. I'm angry that you didn't let me save her. It tore me and my parent apart. My parents seem fine, but I know they miss her. I know I shouldn't question your work, but you know I am, so why? Why did you take her from me? Why couldn't she live? Why did you allow this? I don't like feeling mad at you. It makes me feel even worse than I already do.

Thank you for keeping Joe and me safe. Please help us get safely down the mountain. If I'm not meant to have this guilt, please take it away from me. Did you put Andrea in my life to date? Please forgive me for pulling away and for being angry with you. Please help me to start fresh with you right now.

"You okay? Joe slapped Brent on his back.

Brent shook his head. "I will be."

"Good to hear."

After two days of climbing two different trails, Brent was ready to return. He couldn't focus; this was the wrong mountain to face, unprepared or unfocused. The grace of God kept him alive both days. Andrea had flooded Brent's dreams the last couple of nights. In the first dream, she fell madly in love with him, and they married and lived happily ever after. In the second one, Brent and Andrea experienced go-kart racing, and around corner four, their tires bumped and sent Andrea spinning sideways so fast that the kart flipped over multiple times. Brent had woken up sweating profusely.

Brent couldn't believe he had contemplated getting involved with Andrea. He knew better. Dating Andrea meant putting her in danger, and Brent refused to do that, no matter how he felt about her. Despite his reunion with God, Brent still worried about being unable to protect her. Before bed, he'd read the Bible. He didn't remember where this was, but the notion that no matter how close he was to Andrea, no matter how strong he was, if God didn't want her to be saved, He wouldn't let her be. The same was true with Samantha. He'd had her hand, but God wouldn't let Brent save her - a massive blow to the ego. God wasn't about ego; He detested egos. Bottom line, Brent was scared to love and lose again.

After checking out of their hotel, the guys ate breakfast at the on-site restaurant, The Grand Grille - a cross between elegant and rustic. The floor-to-ceiling windows provided a clear view of the mountain, giving the restaurant a romantic feel, while the sturdy, solid wood tables and wood wall sections behind the bar gave the restaurant a mountain feel. Brent wondered if Andrea would like this place.

Before planning an entire evening away with Andrea, he silently chastised himself. *Stop it! What does it matter? I need to stay away from her.* Brent continued to fuel his inner war with self-doubt, anger, and heartache.

Once the waitress returned with Joe's coffee and Brent's orange juice, Brent slammed his elbows on the table, plopped his hand into his palms, and spilled all the details of his dreams.

After sharing the particulars of his dreams, Joe tapped him on the back, "Look, Man, you are not responsible for Samantha's death; it was not your fault. You're not a murderer. You didn't accidentally kill her; you just couldn't save her. That's not your fault either." Joe rested his hands on the table and continued, "It happened so fast, Man. You need to forgive yourself and move on."

Since the accident, Joe had tried to convince Brent, to no avail, that he couldn't have saved his sister. It had been her time to pass on into Heaven; God's will was more significant than his. Brent had always listened, and to some extent, he agreed, but it always came back - stomach squeezing, heart-wrenching guilt. Guilt for not listening to her that day. Guilt for not getting to her in time. Guilt for yelling at her because she had run ahead. Guilt for pushing his parents and every friend, except for Joe, away after the accident.

Now, he is guilty of not allowing himself to enjoy Andrea, which Joe reminded him is a gift from God.

"Listen, as disastrous as Cherie was, she was a gift too. She taught you what not to go for. Is Andrea anything like Cherie?"

Brent lifted his head, "I think we've moved past the stage of her wanting to turn me to ash with her eyes."

Joe chortled. "Cherie was a fake, heartless human being who doesn't deserve any more of your headspace. Now you can focus on building a meaningful relationship with Andrea." Joe smiled at him to punctuate his statement.

Brent spoke with his hands. "Okay, let's say you're right. Andrea runs hot and cold. I'm not sure she wants to try to have a relationship."

"Ask her," Joe said point blank, just as the waitress brought their steel-cut oatmeal and egg burritos. "Thank you," he said as the waitress placed their food on the table.

Brent felt the physical connection between him and Andrea; he believed she might have felt it, too. They had been flirting with each other that last date, and he'd done nothing but think of her this entire weekend.

"Look, she had told you she'd go out with you, right?" Brent shook his head in agreement. "Then just set it up and see how it goes. You don't have to get married tomorrow, but take one day at a time."

"Thanks, Man!" Brent slowly felt his body relax. He needed to stop thinking for her, bringing himself down. He needed to allow her to share how she was feeling.

For the rest of breakfast, they talked shop. So far, it has been a successful season, and they have had to restock their merchandise, especially their Adventure Park tee shirts and long-sleeved shirts. Donna had booked ten new groups while they had been gone, thanks to the flyers Brent printed and distributed right before leaving.

"We need to hire an office manager to take care of these things." Joe spit out. He'd talked with Brent about this before, but Brent had refused to give any office manager the power to spend his and Joe's money and potentially destroy their business. One thing he'd vividly remembered from Dave when he purchased the park was to keep the heart of the money matters between him and Joe and not to trust outsiders.

Dave had spoken from experience. A few years into running the company, Dave hired an office manager with an accounting background to handle all the ordering, bookings, and accounting, a fatal decision Brent planned to avoid. That thief had robbed Dave blind. He almost had to file for bankruptcy. Fortunately, Dave's wife quit her job at the bank to work with her husband. Within a season, they turned the company around and handled those jobs themselves until they retired.

That got Brent thinking about Andrea. He didn't even know what she did for a living, but would they ever grow close enough, perhaps even marry like Dave and Shirley, and she could run the business side of the operation with him?

"What about Donna? She's running the shop now?" Joe broke into his thoughts. "We could book more groups and work outside like we originally envisioned when we pur-chased the park."

That sounded great to Brent. "Getting away like this is also important, or we'll burn out. Can we table this thought for now? Let's get through this season. We'll make this a priority in the off-season."

The only thing that would make the adventures better would be Donna and Andrea by their sides. Would Andrea be able to give him a chance, let her guard down, and see where this led?

Chapter 11

♥

T HE THRILL OF CLIMBING that wall had lived inside Andrea since her first visit. From that moment on, she'd returned every day to practice and to keep her mind off her upcoming doctor's appointment and Brent. She spent too much time thinking about climbing competitively. She imagined Brent training with her and being at every one of her competitions, cheering her on. Though she hadn't known him long, she believed he'd support her. Then, when she won, or at least finished, Brent could reward her with kisses, sending her into euphoria. Though the kiss he had given her days ago was tender and gentle, unlike the deep, passionate one they experienced on the street outside Guido's, she'd take either one.

Andrea's heart weighed her down. One minute, she'd agonized and stressed over feeling inadequate - not being enough for any man to love, and the next minute, a powerful daydream about being Brent's wife and having his babies, even though they weren't anywhere near that stage, flooded her thoughts. Black circles appeared under her eyes, indicating that she hadn't slept much since Brent left for his climbing trip with Joe.

The idea of the two of them going on an actual date when he returned exhilarated her, but she wondered if it would ever happen. Her focus needed to be on walking again.

Today was a big day. Brent and Joe return, but she must also find out if she will ever walk again. If she could, the entire world would be open to her again. Donna offered to take her, but Brent and Joe were counting on her to be at the park. Admittedly, Andrea would have loved her parents to be there with her, but if that were possible, she wouldn't be in the chair in the first place.

Andrea hadn't expected her doctor's appointment to go as well as it had. Instead of discussing the therapy program, Dr. Chavez shared that an opening for spinal implants was available. Andrea had been put on a long wait list about eight months ago and was now next in line. The exhilarating feeling of being even closer to walking again overwhelmed her.

The way he explained it to her seemed simple enough. Since Andrea's damage was a T6 incomplete spinal cord injury, he could see the surgery being beneficial. Spinal implants were in their early stages, and Andrea would show a considerable act of faith to try this. The doctor provided her with testimonies of three men with spinal cord injuries who had electrodes inserted into their spinal column and a generator set under the skin in their abdomen - long story short; they were able to walk again.

"Bruno, would you even recognize me if I walked?" Her hand glided from the top of Bruno's head to the base of his neck. She never expected him to respond, but he made a noise like a human sigh. She wondered if even Bruno was sick of her.

He'd been her main helper for the past nine months. He turned the lights on and off for her just to show that he could since the switches were about four inches shorter than the standard height. Her contractor worked personally with every subcontractor he hired to ensure she had a house that wouldn't make her feel disabled.

Andrea would love to walk again, but not at a further cost to her health. Was there anything worse that could happen to her during the surgery? Doubtful. Nonetheless, Andrea told Dr. Chavez she needed to pray about it and would get back to him in a couple of days. Thanks to Donna, Andrea started praying again and forgiving God for taking her parents. She'd asked for forgiveness, too, for rejecting him. The Bible verse about knocking and the door opening, asking, and receiving came to her mind.

She fasted lunch and prayed in the spirit of getting a quick answer. God led her to Jeremiah chapter seventeen, verse fourteen. *Heal me, Lord, and I will be healed; save me, and I will be saved, for you are the one I praise.* "Thank you, Lord, for your willingness to heal me," Andrea prayed aloud. "If I don't do the surgery, I'm stuck in this chair the rest of my life. If I had the surgery, I could walk again. Does the risk outweigh the reward?" Andrea sat in silence, waiting.

Listening. The proverbial crickets were all she heard for a long while.

Then, Isaiah chapter thirty-eight popped into her mind. Andrea slowly read through each verse. Near the end, she got her answer. *Lord, by such things, people live, and my spirit finds life in them, too. You restored me to health and let me live. Indeed, it was for my benefit that I suffered such anguish.* "Verses sixteen and seventeen guided her to the phone. Dr. Chavez's office confirmed her decision to have the surgery. The scheduler would call her sometime this week with a date.

As she ended the call, a peace regarding her decision enveloped her.

Donna showed up at Andrea's to have dinner after she closed Adventure Park for the night. "This is why I haven't heard from you as much lately." Donna gestured toward the plethora of DVD sitcoms scattered across Andrea's coffee table.

On the TV screen, Donna recognized the famous couple from the original *Beverly Hills, 90210*. Rolling her eyes, Donna implored, "Could you please move into the Millennium? You're not even old enough to know about most of these shows." Donna picked up the complete series of *Charles in Charge, Gimme A Break, Happy Days, The Facts of Life, Three's Company,* and the originals *Magnum PI and MacGuyver* to make her point.

Andrea's mom loved these shows, and she shared them with Andrea as soon as she felt she could. Andrea picked up *The Golden Girls, Saved by the Bell, Blossom,* and *Laverne and Shirley.* "They don't make shows like this anymore. Today, TV is trash!" Andrea chuckled but meant every word. At least once every month or two, Andrea spent an entire weekend binge-watching the shows she and her parents, but mostly her mom, loved watching together. It helped her feel close to them.

While Andrea loved seeing her friend, it took all her strength to pull herself from living vicariously through Brenda and Dylan's love story to listen to Donna swoon over Joe. "This is a picture of him and Brent at the summit of Mount Washington." Donna pulled her phone back to swipe to another picture and another before she shared one of Joe's texts that invited her to the restaurant the guys ate breakfast at before heading back home this morning. "You and Brent should come with us."

After looking at the pictures and listening to how Joe and Donna plan on progressing in their relationship, Andrea couldn't hold her tongue any longer, "If you like Joe so much, I'm not sure why you are so insistent on pushing Brent and me together. It's not like middle school where your dad would only let you go out if a group of kids were going." The ladies laughed at all the *group outings,* as Donna's dad called them: the school dances, the treks through Baxter State Park, and the Botanical Gardens. Whenever Andrea wasn't with her parents, she and Donna were inseparable.

Andrea's accident had put some distance between them for months since Andrea retreated to her parent's house while contractors built her this house. It wasn't the house of her dreams, but she never dreamed she'd be incapacitated at twenty-four years old. This was a house of necessity rather than desire, yet it grew on Andrea, and now she loved her home. More than ever, Andrea needed to prove to herself she was independent. She never wanted to rely on anyone again. If she couldn't do it herself or with Bruno's help, she wouldn't.

Once the contractor finished her ranch-style home, she put her parent's home on the market. At the time, Andrea felt like she was drowning. Instead of water, a sea of emotions engulfed her. Her parents were the best. Though she was an only child, Andrea had never been lonely. They were like the Three Musketeers. Her parents had instilled in her a love of nature and a desire for adventure. Andrea's mom always said she could pass for a dolphin if she grew a tail. She couldn't recall when she had learned to swim. Andrea always seemed to have known, even though she knew that was impossible. Photos of Andrea and her mom swimming before she learned to walk flooded her mind. The first actual memory Andrea could recollect was right before her fourth birthday. Her parents had taken her to Wells Beach for her first snorkeling adventure.

"Andrea, you need someone in your life," Donna interrupted her thoughts. "Brent seems like a genuinely nice guy." Andrea ultimately agreed, but she couldn't trust that he wouldn't break her heart down the road when he realized she couldn't keep up with the lifestyle he loved and yearned for.

"How can you tell after a few weeks?" Andrea scoffed as she shot her head up toward Donna. "Sorry." Andrea retreated to the sink with her plate almost rolling over Bruno's tail before he leaped out of the way.

Donna followed with hers. "Andrea, you've shut yourself off from living a full life, and I think you're choosing things that are difficult for a paraplegic to complete just to be ... difficult." Donna rinsed her plate and gently set it in the dishwasher, avoiding eye contact with Andrea. "There are so many things you can do, and you don't seem interested in doing them, only the ones you can't. What's going on?"

"Difficult? Seriously! You think I'm being difficult." Andrea dropped a fork that Bruno promptly retrieved. She shoved it in the utensil holder and slammed the dishwasher shut, making Donna jump. "You realize what the last eighteen months have been like for me, right? Andrea didn't want anyone to pity her, but a little understanding would be appreciated. "I lost my family, boyfriend, and use of my legs in the blink of an eye, and you think I'm being difficult." Bruno trotted over and rested his head on Andrea's lap to help calm her. She patted his head, grateful for his presence.

Wow! She thought she knew her best friend. *Apparently not*!

"Why didn't you go to counseling.? You're right. Whatever you've been through is a lot for anyone to deal with, but you're not dealing with it; you are hiding behind old TV sitcoms, good as they may be." Donna laid it all on the table since it's out there now. "You won't talk to me; you won't talk to someone else. First, you shut *everyone* except your contractor out, and now you're either isolating yourself with a television or pushing yourself beyond your limits."

Rubbing Bruno's head helped Andrea exhale and release the tension in her shoulders. She knew Donna was right. She didn't forget about the one night early on when Donna couldn't reach her by phone or by text, so she showed up at Andrea's door and walked into a bloody mess.

Andrea had dropped the dishes she was trying to put in an above-empty cupboard for no other reason than to say she could and did. She cut her forehead and arm before toppling over, trying to avoid the tumbling plates. She couldn't get herself up. Being honest with herself, Andrea knew she hadn't planned on getting up that night. She consciously decided to lie there, hoping she would disappear. If it hadn't been for Donna, she would have slowly bled to death because she didn't have anyone ... *no one* in her life except Donna. But who knows how much longer she would have her now that Donna and Joe were getting all chummy? Andrea didn't want to be a third wheel Donna dragged around...literally.

No, thank you!

God sent us Joe and Brent; whether you want to embrace it or not is your call, but I am. As if just on cue, the alert on Donna's phone stole both ladies' attention.

Andrea knew it was Joe based on how Donna's face lit up like the North Star that led the Shepherds to Baby Jesus.

"A text from Joe." Donna smiled and lifted her shoulders to her ears and down. She read it aloud.

We're back. I'd love to see you! Are you busy?

"You should go, Donna." All Andrea wanted to do was watch TV alone.

Donna shook her head. "Just give me a minute."

While waiting for Donna, Andrea's mind wandered back to the months following her accident. Kyle hadn't even shown up at the hospital for three weeks. When he finally did, he hadn't given a good reason for not being there, but Andrea had been in such shock and grief that she didn't even bother to argue. As the days passed, she had seen him less and less. Then, the day he was supposed to pick her up and take her home, he told her he wouldn't be there and didn't think they would work out. Kyle had thought Andrea wouldn't be able to give him kids or do any more adventures, so he hightailed it out of her life. Kyle deemed Andrea damaged and useless.

Did Brent think the same thing? Stop that, Andrea! She scolded herself. Why does Brent keep stealing my head space? Andrea knew she didn't have to worry so much about her head but rather her heart. Could she be crushing on him and too scared to admit it? Was Donna right?

Days following her discharge from the hospital, she half expected Kyle to call or text since he always did that after acting like a jerk. She forgave him every time and allowed him to neglect or omit her from his plans with his friends. The writing on the wall had become clear: he never loved her. She started to wonder if he even liked her.

"I don't need anyone but you, Bruno," she whispered in his ear so Donna wouldn't hear. "You'll go hiking, sailing, and running or rolling, in my case." During the winter, she'd find something they could do together.

Her heart had never dropped into her stomach when Kyle walked into a room, nor had she felt any fireworks when he intentionally touched her. On the contrary, Andrea's internal temperature rose uncontrollably whenever Brent entered a room. He'd accidentally brushed her arm, and her body acted like it was the Fourth of July! She also couldn't recall a deep yearning to see Kyle. Her desire to see Brent has overwhelmed her the last few days. Now that he was back, she worried about whether or not he would even want to see her. He might have thought about it and realized all he'd miss out on by investing time with her.

Andrea couldn't bear to love and lose again. She was fragile, and her insecurity was high. She feared that If she let herself get any more intrigued with Brent, she'd regret it and end up right back where she was now.

Alone. With her heart in a zillion pieces.

Chapter 12

WHEN HE REALIZED ANDREA chose to stay home and watch television instead of welcoming him home, disappointment rained down on Brent. Even though Donna explained Andrea's conflict, it still stung.

He'd wanted to tell her all about the beautiful foliage that had reminded him of her, vulnerable yet beautiful. The Bullets game he recorded just provided white noise at this point. He needed to know where her head was at.

Brent: Hey. I'm back. How have you been?

He squeezed his eyes shut and tapped the arrow to send the text. It didn't take long for the text alert to return. He pried his eyes open, and his lips instantly lifted like they had a mind of their own. Just seeing her name on the screen increased his blood flow.

Andrea: Good, and you? How was climbing?

Brent wondered if she was just being polite or if she really wanted to hear about the great climbing. He decided to play it safe.

Brent: Is that a true *I'm good,* or a fake one like before? Climbing was good.

Andrea: I'm fine. Watching TV. You?

Brent hadn't experienced a woman who texted with few words. His mom would send paragraphs. He wasn't sure how he felt about this revelation.

Brent: How's your Hollywood Crush? *GIF of Steve Urkel saying "Did I do That?"*

Andrea: What happened to Butler?

Brent: I'm starting to believe that one's true, so I'd rather not think about it.

He knew he was jealous but would never admit that to Andrea.

Andrea: Is someone a little green?

Brent: *Meme of Leonardo Dicaprio from Wolf of Wallstreet – Jealous, Me?*

Andrea: LOL. Sure, okaaaay.

He knew he wasn't believable. Heck, he couldn't even convince himself not to be jealous.

Brent: A thought just came to me. You don't want to tell me because you're ashamed you're crushing on a pretty boy.

Andrea: *emoji laughing face with tears* Definitely not!

Brent: You're right. A pretty boy couldn't handle you.

Andrea: And you think you can?

Their rapid-fire texting was getting heated. Andrea might not like hearing the thoughts he's had of her. Before Brent said something he might regret, he took a second to breathe and then changed the subject.

Brent: How'd your appointment go?

Andrea: Good. Things look promising.

He wasn't sure how far to push, but he wanted more details.

Brent: Promising like you'll be able to walk again? Climb? Etc. Could you give me a few more details, Woman?

He watched and waited for the three dots. They finally appeared. He watched and watched while they wiggled on his screen. Then they disappeared and reappeared three times.

Andrea: Walk, hopefully.

Two words were all he got. "Come on, Woman," Brent spoke to his phone, and Siri's green, red, and blue lights swirled at the bottom of his screen until he pressed the button on the side of his phone for it to disappear.

Brent: Why didn't you want to go to Freddy's tonight?

Andrea: I wanted to be at home with my Hollywood Crush. *emoji wink*

Brent: Funny.

Andrea: Did you want to see me or something?

Brent: I did before that last comment. *emoji smile*

Brent: There's still time if you want. I could come to get you.

He waited a full two minutes for her response.

Andrea: Okay. I'll see you in a few.

Brent: Be there in fifteen.

True to his word, Brent knocked on Andrea's door at quarter past seven. To his surprise, Bruno opened the door for him.

He pushed it open wide and stood next to the door as if he were a human waiting for his guest to cross the threshold, and then he shut the door.

"Thanks, Buddy."

Bruno circled Brent's legs, investigating him. He sniffed his shoes, his legs, and his hands. He must have passed the test because the dog sat on his hind legs until he heard Andrea. When she appeared, Bruno wagged his tail against the stand near the door as she rolled up. "He loves you, doesn't he?"

"Thankfully, someone does." Their eyes locked. Brent thought her eyes had a strangled expression.

"I'm sure if you let more people in, you'd have people loving you more than you think." Brent clamped his mouth shut, but it was too late. Her shocked look probably resembled the one on his face.

"Ready?"

"Yeah. Sorry, I wasn't ready when you got here. I had to finish watching my crush."

Brent tipped his head back and laughed. "You're too much."

When they arrived at Freddy's, Andrea and Brent joined their friends. Joe had his arm draped over Donna's shoulder, and she snuggled into his side. Before entering the restaurant, Brent spied Joe and Donna in the window as he walked by. They weren't sitting as close as they are now, and Joe didn't have his arm around her. He shrugged off an inkling pestering his gut.

"Care if we join you?" Joe's head jerked up at the sound of Brent's voice. Donna bounced in her seat and clapped her hands together when she saw Andrea.

"Hey, Buddy." Joe reached out his hand, gripped Brent's, and pulled him into his shoulder. "I'm glad you came." Then Joe turned to Andrea. "Thanks for getting him here. I tried, and twenty years of friendship wasn't enough to pull him from the game."

Brent couldn't remember a time when he'd enjoyed himself more. They shared stories, and he watched Andrea's eyes light up when she smiled or laughed at Joe's silliness. The best part was when she blushed after Brent complimented her or "accidentally" brushed the tips of his fingers on her forearm.

The next thing he knew, the ladies listened intently to Joe share potentially life-altering events from their trip to New Hampshire. "And there we were picking wild berries, thinking we had hit the jackpot when we came face to face with a black bear on its hind legs."

Donna rested one hand on Joe's as her other hand covered her gaping mouth, "What did you do."

Nonchalantly, Joe waved off any concern with his hand, "We let it have the berries and ate our protein packs." That got a roar from everyone at the table.

Brent peered at Andrea from the corner of his eye and noticed her smile. His heart felt like a novice acrobat attempting all the challenging flips yet stumbling through them all. On the way back from New Hampshire, he promised to ask

Andrea out and see where it led, but he didn't quite know how to start that conversation.

He'd played it out in his head a couple of times. *Hey, Andrea, I know we got off to a bad start, and I don't have a solid record of being able to protect women who are important to me, but would you like to take a chance on me?* His other futile attempts didn't sound much better.

After returning from the restroom to gain his composure, the guys paid the bill. Donna and Joe announced they wanted to take an evening stroll to enjoy the cool autumn weather that arrived before the calendar declared the season. "Do you want to join us?"

"Nah, we'll figure something out." Brent promptly answered for both of them.

A pink hue assaulted Andrea's cheeks again. He wasn't sure what she thought he meant, but it hadn't been what he was now thinking. *God, please reign my thoughts in. I will honor you and stay out of a woman's bed until she's my wife. Please help me keep my eyes on you.*

Before leaving, Joe hugged Brent and pulled his buddy toward him, slapping Brent's back. "You got this," Joe assured his friend before bidding Andrea adieu.

Meanwhile, Donna hugged Andrea and spoke into the side of her face, "Give him a chance. See where this goes." Brent tried to avoid eye contact with her so Andrea didn't think he was eavesdropping. However, he'd be sure to thank Donna later.

On the way to his truck, Brent apologized, "I'm sorry this keeps happening." When Andrea didn't say anything immediately, he worried she was upset.

But then she smirked, "Sorry for what, wanting to be alone with me, yet too afraid to speak up, leaving it up to your best friend to do your dirty work."

Brent plastered one palm over his heart and his other hand on top of his first one, pretending like he'd die from her words. "Ouch, that really hurt."

"Truth hurts!" Andrea laughed and shrugged one shoulder up and down.

Brent countered with a smile, "I see. Well, your warm and fuzzy personality chased off the gentleman inside me."

"Touché. Sorry," Andrea half smiled in embarrassment. "I guess it's been harder to adjust than I care to admit."

"Of course it has. I was kidding with you." Brent balanced on the balls of his feet and rested his hand on her arm, sending electrodes through his arm. He thought his chamois shirt would have acted like a buffer; it hadn't.

"Every *just kidding* has a little bit of truth to it. Andrea reasoned. "It's okay, you weren't wrong. I've been prickly since my accident."

"Do you feel like strolling through the park across the street, or would you rather I take you home?" He hoped she wanted to spend more time with him.

"I'd love the fresh air if you're up for it." Andrea declared with a beaming smile.

Once they reached the other side of the street, Brent stuffed his hands in his pockets. He played one of his favorite games to get to know her better.

"Would you rather be in a room with a snake or a mouse?" Brent began.

"Neither would bother me because the snake would eat the mouse, and I'd leave the room."

Brent burst out laughing. "Not a fan of either."

"Not a fan, but not afraid either. Snakes give me more of the willy's than a mouse does. My dad watched a Chuck Norris movie with me when I was a kid, and a guy put a mouse, well rat, in a bag and tied it around Chuck Norris's head to torture him, so I'd prefer not to be in close quarters with the rodent." Andrea explained.

"Okay, your turn. Would you rather mountain climb or water ski?" Andrea questioned.

"Ooh, good one." Brent rubbed his chin, contemplating his answer. "I love them both, but I'd have to say mountain climbing; it's more of a thrill." Once he answered, he felt guilty, remembering that Andrea had dreamed of climbing Knife's Edge not too long ago. He didn't apologize for his answer. Brent recalled Donna's warning: *Do not apologize for things you can do that she can't. That will make it worse for her. If you have to, pretend she can do everything you talk about. Trust me.*

"You're turn," Andrea encouraged.

Brent sported the cat that ate the canary smile as he studied Andrea's face. "Would you rather go on a date with Gerald Butler or me?"

"What?! This again. He's not my Hollywood crush."

"Great, looks like I stand a chance." Brent smiled.

"I guess you do," Andrea stated bluntly.

Brent froze while Andrea continued to wheel on. Chasing after her, he turned and stopped directly in front of her, using his arms to stop her rolling. "Are you serious?"

"Are you?" Andrea countered.

"Yeah, I'm serious. As a matter of fact, I think our first date should be right now. Let's head to Gloria's for an ice cream cone."

"That could work, or we could go back to my house and have Ben and Jerry's in my freezer. I keep multiple flavors in case of an emergency."

Brent cracked up, "Do you have many ice cream emergencies?"

With a stone face, she replied, "Not as many as I used to." When she smiled, Brent returned the gesture, feeling his heart balloon to double its size.

When he lifted Andrea into his truck this time, Brent felt different. Her closeness ripped at every part of his body, and he wanted to kiss her. He even leaned in toward her delectable-looking lips but didn't trust himself, so he kissed her cheek and continued to tease her, "I know I'm no Gerald Butler, but thank you for giving this dog his day."

As he put her wheelchair in the back, she whispered aloud, "Dog, ya right. You're better than Butler any day."

After hopping in the driver's seat, he wasted no time returning to their game. "Would you rather go to the Caribbean or Hawaii?"

"That's easy," Andrea's bright smile lit up the cab. "Hawaii. I flew to the Caribbean for my sixteenth birthday with my parents. We stayed there for a week and then started a two-week cruise from there. I loved it, but Hawaii is my bucket list item."

"Me, too." A microburst of excitement spread through his chest at the thought of visiting Hawaii with the woman, making his truck smell like the paradise they both wanted to explore.

She didn't say anything or show any emotion. The tense silence inside the cab weighed on Brent like a boulder in the pit of his stomach. "I really like you!" He blurted out and took a second to catch his breath. His heart nearly leaped out of his chest and bounced off the steering wheel. His white knuckles continued to grip the wheel as he turned into Andrea's driveway. Every passing second of silence convinced him that he should have kept his mouth shut!

Chapter 13

♥

ANDREA JUMPED WHEN BRENT slammed his door shut with too much force. She heard him say sorry as he walked toward the tailgate. Still in shock when he opened the door, she barely felt him pick her up, but being so close to him sent shockwaves to her brain. She looked intently into his eyes as his arms embraced her. For a brief moment, she felt like her body fit perfectly in the crease of his arm and shoulder. She brought her other arm up and wrapped it around his neck. Andrea scanned his lips as he parted them ever so slightly with his tongue. It was like the two of them were frozen in time. She pulled him closer to her as she leaned in for a sweet, gentle kiss. The moment their lips touched, Brent let out a slight moan from the back of his throat.

Andrea traced her fingers down Brent's chiseled jaw and rested her palm on his chest. She felt his heart throbbing. It matched hers. Additionally, hers fluttered like a million butterflies landed right before the kiss and then took off in unison. Andrea wasn't sure what this kiss meant, but there was one thing she knew for sure: Brent's kisses were an addictive drug, pulling her in deeper and deeper.

Bruno welcomed Andrea home, pounding his tail against the stand near the door (a staple move for him) as she rolled by. Brent offered to help with the ice cream, but she politely declined. She welcomed him to keep her company in the kitchen while she retrieved it.

Andrea rattled off the Ben and Jerry's flavors nestled deep in her freezer. "Phish Food, Mint Chocolate Chance, Netflix, Half Baked, Chunky Monkey, and New York Super Fudge Chunk."

"How many emergencies can one girl have?" Brent winked at Andrea. "Where are the bowls and spoons? I'll grab those." Brent offered.

"Are you serious? You don't eat Ben and Jerry's out of a bowl. Come choose." Andrea ordered. While she never did eat Ben and Jerry's from a bowl, she had another reason for not wanting Brent to get the dishes.

All of the above-head cupboards were empty. Andrea made her contractor build them for appearance. Additionally, right after her accident, Andrea was determined to walk again, so she thought the higher cupboards would be necessary. To date, they hadn't been used.

Everything she needed lived in all her cupboards below her counter space. Seeing Brent bend down to get something that would typically be in an upper cupboard embarrassed her.

"Well, I can't eat this all right now after that dinner." He rested his palm on his stomach.

"You don't think I'm eating all of mine, do you? Looks like you'll have to come back another time to finish it with me." Andrea's flirtatious voice filled the room.

"Wow! Andrea, this is a spacious kitchen. I imagine there are chefs out there who'd like this much counter space."

She enjoyed the pleasure in his voice as she had designed the space. A six-foot countertop with cupboards underneath was stationed to the right of the refrigerator, and it acted more like an appliance holder. She needed more low cupboards, so there are outlets all along that backsplash for her juicer, blender, air fryer, and mixer. If she ever had a party, it would be the ideal place to lay out the food. Her table took up the space about four feet in front of it, just enough for Andrea's wheelchair to pass by.

She finally made it to the freezer drawer. "Which one would you like?" Perhaps this was a bit much. Maybe through Brent's eyes, her freezer looked like the ice cream section in a grocery store with all the ice cream cartons neatly organized so one could see the ice cream flavors to make a quick selection. *Oh well, now he knows my weakness.*

"What are you having?" Brent questioned. "I don't want to take your favorite emergency ice cream."

"Tonight, I'm in the mood for Mint Chocolate Chance. How about you?"

"I'd like to try Chunky Monkey, but I don't want to waste it if I don't like it," Brent spoke aloud.

Andrea tossed him the pint. "If you don't like it, try something else. I'll still eat it. Ice cream doesn't get wasted in this house." Andrea assured him with a smile.

Back in the living room, Andrea tried to clean up her coffee table, but Brent, like Donna, found her eighties and nineties television shows comical. "I haven't even heard of some of these shows, *Night Court, Perfect Strangers.*" Brent held them up, questioning their authenticity or something. He picked up two different cases and said, "Okay, I have heard of *Growing Pains* and *Full House.* What do we have here? Your fake Hollywood crush." Brent held up *Family Matters and then* set it, along with the others, back on the table, avoiding Andrea's ice cream that she had set down so she could transfer to the couch.

Brent waited for her to settle and then passed her the ice cream from the table. He sat next to her on the couch, close enough that his woodsy smell assaulted her senses, making her keenly aware of his presence.

She encouraged Brent to try his ice cream. Before he even swallowed the first bite, she inquired, "What do you think?"

Waiting until he entirely consumed his first bite, he looked to the sky like he needed to analyze the ice cream to determine if he liked it. Based on his smile, Andrea knew that he already had his answer; he just wanted to tease her. "It's pretty good. Thank you." Brent said.

"I thi–

"Bre–"

They both stopped mid-word to let the other continue. When neither of them did, Brent insisted, "Ladies first."

That simple gesture made Andrea melt from the inside out. "Brent, I'm afraid of whatever this is." Andrea waved her spoon back and forth between the two of them. "I don't know if Donna told you how I got here," pointing at the empty wheelchair.

"No, she said you might tell me someday." A pang of delight through her. "I'd love to hear the story whenever you're ready."

Andrea loved hearing that Donna respected her and her story. Her nerves got the better of her, and she started swirling her spoon around, breaking the ice cream down from a hard solid to a soft, stirred-up texture. "Eighteen months ago, my parents and I were driving home from the first mud run I had participated in." Andrea left her spoon in the container and started to pick at the hole in her jeans. "Long story short, a drunk driver struck us head-on. When the police pulled me out of the car using the jaws of life, the rescue crew strapped me to a backboard. As they wheeled me toward the ambulance, I saw two bodies on the ground with black tarps over them. My parents were both killed upon impact. At that moment, I didn't realize I couldn't feel anything below the waist, but now I remember a look the EMTs shared when they conducted their field testing; I couldn't feel whatever they did from my waist down."

"I'm so sorry, Andrea. I assume you were close with your parents."

"They were my best friends. I spent just as much time with them as I do Donna."

Brent placed one arm over the back of the couch and the other on her knee despite not being able to feel his hand on her knee like most people would. She knew it was there, and the gesture released a giddiness she hadn't felt since her first crush in high school.

"I hate it when someone has to endure the consequences of another person's poor decision." Brent stared at her so intently that she felt his emotions. He wanted to kiss her; she could tell. As he leaned closer, she recognized his dilated pupils, and his hand had traveled to her hip, resting there for the time being. A kiss would be wonderful right now, but if she was going to see if Brent could genuinely be interested in her – wheelchair and all. She needed to get everything out in the open.

She leaned back to continue sharing, and she noticed the disappointment in his eyes. Maybe that was a sign, or the *sign* she needed to know he was interested. After telling him about Kyle and his disappearance while in the hospital, she revealed that she never loved the guy. She chalked it up to bad timing and a bruised ego. "He never made me feel the way..." Andrea looked down at her jeans and began slowly ripping small pieces of thread at the hole to avoid finishing that sentence.

Brent leaned closer and lifted Andrea's chin with his thumb. He gazed at her with an endearing smirk, "Finish what you were going to say, please."

Gazing into his eyes, she whispered, "He never made me feel the way I do when I'm with you."

"No one has ever made me feel like you do when I'm around you, either." He leaned in for a second fantastic kiss, but Andrea's palms created two walls on his chest, pushing him back.

"Never?"

"Never," he whispered near her ear and kissed her cheek."

The goosebumps on Andrea's bare arms sent shivers right through her. Andrea blamed it on the ice cream. Yeah. There's no way any human being could make another person feel this alive.

"Thank you for sharing your story with me. You should introduce me to Kyle so I can thrash him."

Andrea tipped her head back and let out an authentic laugh. She hadn't felt this good since before her accident. "Thank you, but trust me, he's not worth it."

"Don't sell yourself short. You're worth more than that." Brent caressed his knuckles on her cheek and slid closer to her, pressing their thighs tight to each other. He placed his hands on either side of her face and gently tilted her head. "Andrea, I want to kiss you, not to make a point to an old girlfriend, but I *want* to show you that I really like you."

His admission shocked her. She was speechless. His milk chocolate eyes were fixed on her, causing her insides to melt into a gooey mess.

"Is it okay if I kiss you, Andrea?" The sound of her name rolling off his lips sounded perfect like she could hear him say it for the rest of her life.

Finding her voice, she let out a whimper, "Yes."

That was all he needed. Brent claimed her lips. It proved to be too much for Andrea. She let out a whimper, encouraging Brent to pull her on his lap and deepen the kiss. Her hands roamed over his chest, where she felt the thumping of his heart. Erratic, like hers. Then her hands traveled to his shoulders before one moved to the soft stubble fixed on his jaw. Oh man, what a strong jaw lay beneath her fingers. Brent pulled back slightly and dropped kisses along her jawline to the spot just below her ear. In the absence of his lips, Andrea let out a little groan. Her desire for Brent's lips to return grew - if even for just a brief moment. It would be heavenly to taste the banana and chocolate flavoring left behind from his ice cream. She equated that to *a cherry on top* mentality.

This kiss overwhelmed Andrea in a good way. As Brent's lips made their way back up the same path they'd just paved, Andrea let Brent continue with his take-charge demeanor. Their lips tangoed together once more. Andrea lost all sense of time and space. Her hands celebrated as they roamed over the bumps and ridges in his chest and shoulders. For a fleeting moment, she'd even forgotten her disability until her brain registered the legs' desire to move but couldn't. *Would she be enough for Brent?*

That thought forced Andrea to pull away. She brushed her fingers along the length of her swollen lips. "I think we should cool it before it's too late."

"Will you help me off?" Andrea motioned to her now empty place on the couch.

Brent grinned. "You're making progress."

"What?"

"You asked for help," Brent clarified.

"Lapse in judgment, I suppose." Andrea beamed.

Brent lifted Andrea easily to her spot on the couch. "What's distracting you?" He raised an eyebrow at her. What was he waiting for her to admit, that his kiss had sent her to the moon and back?

"Perhaps we should watch a movie. Maybe a superhero? Do you have a favorite one?" Andrea inquired.

Brent narrowed his eyes at her. She dipped her head. "You clearly have a favorite one. I'm going to learn your Hollywood crush, aren't I?"

"Lemme guess, now that I have a more narrow topic. It's got to be Iron Man."

"Excellent guess, but no."

Brent put his forefinger to his chin. "Is it Captain America?"

"Another great guess, still no."

Seconds tick by. "Oh, what was I thinking? It's Thor."

A little giggle escaped Andrea. "Nope, but the amount of muscle is definitely closer."

Brent flexed his biceps. "So they look more like this?"

Andrea let out a gust of air, masking a spontaneous laugh. "Oh, there's nothing wrong with your muscles. No compar- ison for sure." She wrapped her hands around his biceps, unable to touch her fingers. "What great muscles you have." Andrea winked at him.

"I don't know anyone with muscles like Thor...besides me." Andrea loved this new teasing confidence in Brent. It was in a word...sexy.

"Try another superhero brand." Andrea hinted.

Brent's eyebrows formed a V, showing his confusion. "What is there besides Marvel?"

"DC," Andrea stated, almost appalled that he wasn't up on his superheroes. Though if she was in the mood for confessional, she'd have to admit that Brent was a superhero in his own way and, at this point, the only one who'd help her forget her love of them.

"Batman?" shock pierced his voice.

Andrea passed him the remote. "Here, push play."

Brent sat straight back, wide eyes glued on the television. She could tell the anticipation was eating away at him. After the open credits, the title appeared with a bass drum to make its mark. He slowly turned his head, jaw slightly dropped. "Are you serious? What does he have that I don't have?"

Nothing that came to mind at the moment. Andrea shrugged her shoulders and nodded. Undeniably, she'd become somewhat infatuated with the man sitting beside her. He reminded her of her own real-life Aquaman. One of the things that made both of them so appealing to her was that they didn't think they were bewitching. They both recognized that they had fantastic, mouth-watering muscles, yet they discounted all their other great features, such as being protective and kind.

Brent cleared his throat, bringing her focus off his muscles and to his eyes. Those weren't any less distracting. Like a magician, his gaze could hypnotize her. Chills ran rapidly through her upper half.

"You are way more beautiful th—"

"—I am not beautiful." Brent scoffed.

"Says you."

The corner of Brent's lips pulled towards his ears. "Women are beautiful."

"I get it; you're not man enough to be called beautiful. You'd rather have handsome, hunky, alluring—"

He cut her off again. "Woman, I am man enough for you to call me beautiful if *you* want. I don't see it, and you better not say it in front of anyone else. I'd thrash someone for less than that."

"Are you saying you'd thrash me?" Andrea rested her hand on her hip, sitting as straight as possible to make herself look bigger, but he dwarfed her.

Like in the movies, Brent leaned in so slowly that Andrea's insides ached with anticipation. The determination in his eyes had her stomach doing backflips. He stopped an inch from her lips, their breath mingled before he brushed his knuckles down her cheek and whispered, "I'd never hurt you, Andie."

Andie. He called me Andie. No one other than Donna and her parents had called her Andie. For whatever reason, that name on his lips was akin to Cupid's arrow - it pierced her heart. She whispered, "I know." her palms pressed against his chest and glided around his neck. She closed the minuscule gap between their lips.

She hadn't given him a chance to say any more sweet statements or to tease her. The moan that came from the back of his throat let her know that he didn't mind. This was the kind of thrashing she'd take from him any time.

But then, without warning, something hit him. She'd seen the shift in his eyes but hadn't known where it came from. He stood up, said goodbye, and left. What had she done wrong?

<h1 style="text-align:center">Chapter 14</h1>

♥

THE FOLLOWING DAY, BRENT swung his legs to the side of the bed, brushed his hand through his hair, and pushed off the mattress when a pounding at his door made him jump. He rushed out of his bedroom toward the door, "Who is it?" shock evident in his voice.

"Open up, Buddy, it's me!"

Swinging the door open, "What do you want, Joe?"

"Aw, grumpy this morning, I see. Joe slapped a white bag with a big pink and brown Wilma's Bakery sticker at Brent's chest, pushing him aside and taking two long strides into Brent's home.

Brent grunted.

"Man, you look like something the cat dragged in. Get yourself together; we're going out."

Brent dropped his hand and walked toward the couch, "Nope, not today." I'm watching the game I had to record last night." Brent plopped on the couch, recalling how he had let himself get carried away when Andrea had kissed him. The sweet taste of her silky lips sent shivers down his spine, and the ocean's cottony smell that enveloped her still permeated his senses. She had shared her accident. That was the perfect time to share his past, yet he hadn't. They'd kissed, which was great. But as he looked into her innocent eyes, he'd seen his inability to protect her. That's where he and Aquaman were different. Aquaman was a superhero... a made-up one, but still.

Brent had just left her house. Disappeared. She probably wondered what she'd done wrong. She internalized everything. That made him the biggest coward known to man.

Her kisses were mind-blowing, so he couldn't take all the fault for getting lost in them and not sharing his past, right? *No. It's not her fault.* Brent didn't even realize that Joe was gabbing away until he felt a hard punch in the arm, bringing him back to reality.

"Did you hear me? We're going to The Cove; let's go."

"Did you hear me? I said, no."

"We're meeting Donna and Andrea." Joe held Andrea's name longer to capture Brent's attention.

"Does Andrea know I'm coming?" Brent asked.

"Yeah, why? What happened last night?" Joe questioned as he walked to Brent's refrigerator and grabbed a soda.

"Nothing I'm going to share. She commented that you always make plans for her and me." Brent admitted. "You've got to give me a chance to ask her occasionally."

"Sorry, Man. Does that mean you're going to start asking?"

"I'd like to. She told me about her accident." He paused. Joe's searching eyes urged him to continue. "Instead of sharing my accident with her, I left, never acknowledging how I lost Samantha.

Joe shut the refrigerator door and popped the top on the soda can. He gulped half the can in one shot. "You must know by now that losing Samantha was God's will, not your fault. You've punished yourself long enough. No one, except you, has ever blamed you for Sammy's death."

Brent began to argue that the newspapers did, but Joe brushed that off, deeming the reporters who did were nothing more than gossip rag wannabes who probably were unemployed journalists at this very moment.

"I've heard this many times," Brent mumbled.

'When are you going to start listening then?" Joe's irritated tone wasn't lost on Brent.

Brent shook his head and shrugged. "It's a bitter pill to swallow.

Usually, Joe would appease him and talk about Samatha as long as he wanted, but not today. "Go get dressed. We should stop at the sub shop for sandwiches."

"Can we stop at the store so I can make Andrea one of those salads instead? She doesn't eat subs." Joe's grin irked him.

"What!?" Brent asked.

"Interesting, you know what she'll eat and what she won't eat, but you won't admit that you have feelings for her at all." Joe sounded more like an annoying younger brother than he did his friend.

Brent threw the couch pillow at his best friend, who knew him too well. "We've talked. I listened. It's nothing."

It was definitely something. Andrea had taken up his dreams and his daydreams. He'd made so many plans for them in his head that he'd lost track.

"Hey, I pay attention to what is important to me, too," Joe countered. "Donna's beautiful sea-blue eyes, long slender legs, and big, bright smile. Joe squeezed the couch pillow too much for Brent's liking. He told him to take his fantasies someplace else as he ripped the pillow from Joe's arms, throwing it back on his couch.

The thought of seeing Andrea today caused an endless pit in his stomach. He had no business getting all excited over a woman who would eventually deem him a deplorable human being for killing his only sister. The bitter sting of regret overpowered Brent. Regret that he couldn't save his sister. Regret that he let Andrea get as close as she did. *What a mess!*

He couldn't admit his failure. It had cost him so much. " Joe, I just left yesterday. She's probably mad at me about that. Besides, she'll never understand my past."

"Don't make her mind up for her. Tell her and let her decide what she can understand and what she can't. Remember how mad she got at Guido's telling us how we assumed so many things about her? I wouldn't do that again."

Joe placed his hand on Brent's shoulders. "Look, Man, I am here for you. I tell you this from the bottom of my heart. You're being an idiot."

Brent pushed out a breath and shook his head.

"You need to tell her. If she doesn't understand, then you have your answer. You can go back to being boring,

Brent, watching the Boston Bullets yourself. If she does understand, you can begin to build a relationship with this woman. It's written all over your face that you like her, but I don't see any lip gloss this time." Joe slapped both of Brent's shoulders before heading for the door. "Let's go."

Thirty minutes later, the guys were heading to Andrea's house in Brent's beast. He smiled every time he thought of Andrea calling his truck that. Joe admitted that he and Donna conjured up the beach plan last night after Andrea called Donna, upset that Brent had left without any explanation. Donna had told Joe that this brought Andrea back to doubting her worth again, so they couldn't let too much time get in the way, or Andrea may never feel worthy.

Guilt raked through his body hearing that. He'd caused more pain to a woman he cared about. When would he stop doing that? When he asked his dad this years ago, he'd told Brent, "Never." At the time, the men had chuckled at his answer, but Brent hadn't found it as comical now that the statement had a whole lot of truth to it.

When he pulled his truck into Andrea's yard, he saw Bruno sitting at attention on the top porch step. With the front door wide open, Brent could see the ladies inside. He was happy that Bruno had warmed up to him, but he wondered if the dog had sensed Andrea's mood change after he left last night and if Bruno would hold him accountable now.

"Look, Bruno is guarding that door. Think he'll let us in?" Brent asked.

"You try first." Joe chuckled.

Meanwhile, Donna sat on Andrea's couch, still trying to convince her what a great idea it was to spend this beautifully warm September day at The Cove. "Look, the guys are here. Come with us. You know that the water makes you feel alive. Talk to him. Find out why he left. Donna told Andrea that she could even bring Bruno if she wanted. Donna heard a vehicle pull into Andrea's driveway.

Moments later, Donna appeared on the porch. Joe nearly fell out of the truck, looking at Donna. "Isn't she gorgeous?"

"What are you telling me for?" Brent scoffed, "Tell her." He slapped Joe's chest with the back of his hand right before Joe hopped out.

Joe hugged Donna. Then she grabbed his hand, leading Joe to Brent's truck. He rolled down the window, but his smile faded when Donna didn't greet him with one of her own. "What's up?

"I can't convince Andrea to come with us. Your leaving last night bothered her. It set her back."

Brent killed the engine and started to open the door, so Joe and Donna moved out of the way. "Let me go talk to her. Is Bruno going to let me in?" Brent strolled up the driveway, talking to Bruno all the while. "Hey Bruno. You watching out for our girl." He didn't budge. Brent could see how seriously Bruno took his job, like the guards at Buckingham Palace.

Thankfully, Bruno let him pass. When he reached the top step, Brent paused briefly, taking in Andrea's beauty. Her light brown hair, pulled to one side of her neck, cascaded down her shoulder. That left the side of her neck closest to him exposed. That set his mind ablaze, imagining how soft her skin would feel if he could get close enough.

Brent shook the thoughts from his head and lightly rapped on the open door. "Hey, can I come in?"

Andrea met his eyes. He saw pools of pain that ripped at his heart, knowing he'd caused it. "Sure."

"I am so sorry I bolted out of here last night. It had nothing to do with you. I have my own past to deal with." He paused, not wanting to show all his weaknesses upfront. Brent continued, "The thought of sharing it ..." He shook his head again to stifle his emotion. "... and you being disgusted with me... it was something I couldn't bear." Brent knelt before Andrea and rested his hands over both of hers. Please come with us to the beach. Afterward, we can talk just the two of us?"

He could see her contemplating it for a moment. "We shouldn't waste a beautiful day at the beach just because you're a wuss," she reasoned. Brent couldn't help but chuckle at her teasing. "Okay, let's go."

Brent lifted her off the couch and into her chair. She let out a cute little squeal. "I wasn't expecting that." She wrapped her arms around his neck. Chills ran down his spine when her fingertips brushed the skin on his neck.

"You should have. I want to carry you everywhere." Brent loved the way Andrea gazed at him. Perhaps it was admiration. He wasn't sure, but he wanted her to look at him like that for a long time.

Brent opened the back door of his truck to let Bruno hop in. "Good boy." Brent encouraged the dog.

"I can drive if you don't want dog hair in your truck or don't feel like lifting me into your truck." The twinkle in her eye caught Brent's attention.

"I thought you wanted Bruno to come?"

Andrea nodded. "I enjoy taking him places with me. But I planned on driving." She pointed to her SUV in the garage. "I had the dealership install a custom push/pull handle on the steering wheel that controls acceleration and braking."

"I'm good driving. Besides, the seats are leather. I can wipe them down if the hair bothers me."

"I get it. You need this massive three-quarter-ton truck to stretch out your legs. I figured you were sick of lifting me in and out of the truck."

"Never. I'm Brent Smith, heavy lifter at your service."

Andrea's mouth dropped as she let out a breath, "Seriously?!"

Brent dropped his head and rushed to open his truck's passenger side door, explaining that it came out wrong. He didn't mean it. "I'm sorry."

That hadn't stopped her teasing him when he got in the truck. When Brent hopped in the driver's side, she put on her best-frustrated face, stifling her laugh. "I didn't hurt those big, beautiful muscles, did I, Mr. Heavy Lifter? I'd hate to be responsible for any injury you might have endured from lifting me into the truck." When she couldn't contain her laughter any longer, she burst out, "You should see your face; it's sweet how concerned you look."

Brent's cheeks flushed. "You think I'm sweet and have beautiful muscles. Huh, that's just what every guy likes to hear." Brent's smile lit up Andrea's heart. "Didn't we talk about this?'

"Yes, we did. You are beautiful. I didn't say I'd stop saying that. I agreed not to say it in front of people. Bruno can't talk, so he won't make fun of you."

Brent did like to hear Andrea's descriptions of him. Maybe not *beautiful,* but he felt that name was here to stay. He wasn't sure how he felt about being called sweet either. Every woman loves a sweet man, right? What every woman thought didn't matter to him; he only cared what Andrea thought. Brent grabbed the steering wheel to steady himself. Turning his head toward Andrea, he gazed at her, shook his head, and chuckled. Unable to think straight, that was all he could do now.

For most of the ride to the beach, Andrea shared a skiing story of when she first started competing. Brent laughed harder than he had in years.

"Twelve years ago, with knees slightly bent in the ready position, I shot off the start line and gained speed quickly as I roared down the mountain. When I approached the first jump, my ski hit something that sent me in the air before the jump. My arms flailed out wide with poles jammed in the palm of my hands."

"You're joking, right?"

Andrea shook her head. "My crash landing was anything but graceful. One ski flew off my boot; the other poked into the mountain briefly—just long enough to twist my knee. Upon impact, I tumbled down the mountain in repeated somersaults until I abruptly stopped."

She broke into the movie playing in his mind, "It's a riot now,' she lightly swatted his shoulder," "but at the time, not only was I utterly humiliated, I damaged my knee and couldn't ski for the rest of the season."

"I'm sorry." Brent put a hand to his chest, trying to stifle his laugh.

Finally, they arrived at the beach. After getting Andrea into her chair, Brent opened the back door for Bruno. To his surprise, Bruno hadn't run around all excited. Instead, he trotted over to Andrea and sat next to her. She rewarded him with a rub behind his ears.

The two couples and Bruno tossed the frisbee for a long time. Andrea smiled when Brent threw the frisbee to Bruno, who ran, leaped, and caught it! Then he trotted it to her, leaving Brent about ten yards away with his hands lifted, palms up, calling Bruno a traitor.

With Bruno leading the pack, the four of them hiked one of the trails her chair could trek over the easiest. This may not be the strenuous climbing Brent was used to, but he couldn't imagine being elsewhere.

"Give your arms a rest." Brent pushed Andrea's chair for her the rest of the trail. "Did you know they make wheelchairs that can be pushed through the sand?"

"No. How do you know that?" Andrea angled her neck to the side and back, searching for his face.

Brent shrugged. "I looked it up."

When they finished the trail, Brent suggested they go kayaking.

"Yes." Joe pumped his fist.

Brent and Joe had the double kayaks ready to launch ten minutes later. Donna was situated in front with her life jacket securely clipped around her. Once Joe got in, they were off, paddling around the ocean.

He'd have to get used to everyone staring at him. It annoyed him. He could see why Andrea didn't like to go out. Brent shifted so that the gawkers couldn't directly view Andrea. He carried her to the kayak while Joe took her chair to the waterfront and sat beside Bruno. Nothing would happen to her chair with him guarding it. Bruno was amazing. He sat on his hind legs at the water's edge, protecting Andrea's wheelchair and eyeing the kayak wherever it traveled. Bruno was the best lifeguard ever. He didn't doubt that Bruno would come to the rescue if she fell into the water. Of course, he would try to save Andrea, but with his track record, he appreciated Bruno's potential help.

Brent's stomach growled ferociously. They had worked up an appetite. Bruno waited well-mannered as Brent pushed the kayak towards shore. To his surprise, Bruno bounded over the small waves, secured the rope in his mouth, and pulled Andrea the rest of the way.

"Good boy." Brent rubbed Bruno's head.

Donna and Joe arrived back at that point. They disembarked quickly. Joe pulled in the kayak while Donna brought Andrea's chair out of the sand.

Brent lifted Andrea from the kayak, carrying her across the sand and to her chair. "Thank you."

Andrea reached out for Bruno, who cantered to her side. "Thank you for the ride, buddy." Andrea put both hands on either side of Bruno's snout and rubbed his ears while she kissed his wet nose."

"I helped push, and I carried you." Brent gave her a sad pout, pushing his bottom lip out.

"Come here." Andrea requested.

When Brent got close enough, she asked him to kneel momentarily. She placed both her hands on Brent's cheeks and repeated herself. "Thank you for the push. Thank you even more for carrying me." She rubbed her fingertips through his scalp right above his ears. "You're a good boy." Then she pulled him forward and kissed his nose.

"Are you through?"

Andrea chuckled, "I think so."

After fanning out the blanket, Brent put their bag on one corner and sweatshirts on the other three to prevent the wind from blowing them. After setting out the cooler and bag of food, Brent lifted Andrea to the picnic.

"Thank you for transferring me everywhere." Andrea's hand on his neck kicked his heart rate up a few notches.

Brent sat on the blanket next to Andrea. "It's my pleasure. Thank you for letting me carry you."

"Trust me, you'll get sick of it. Heck, I don't even want to transfer myself that much. I certainly wouldn't blame you if you got sick of lugging my rear end everywhere."

Brent blushed at her words. *Why? She never should have referred to any of her body parts. How's a man supposed to think straight when women talk like that?* "Don't worry; you just need to sit back and let me carry you anywhere and everywhere you need to go."

He enjoyed watching the color rise on her cheeks.

Brent fed Bruno treats. Based on Andrea's smile, he could tell she enjoyed watching him and Bruno get along together. Around Andrea, his heart was a chocolate lava cake. He hoped their conversation later would go as smoothly as the day. What could possibly go wrong?

Chapter 15

♥

CONVERSATION ON THE WAY home continued easily for both of them. Andrea found herself laughing so hard that tears fell from her eyes. Her lungs silently begged for oxygen. Andrea watched Brent's muscles shift in different places every time he moved his arms as he talked. She shared her few triathlon experiences and listened intently when Brent re-lived the trouble he had had during his first sprint triathlon. "It's really embarrassing because I know I could have finished better, but I was doomed from the start," Brent shook his head.

"I'm sure it couldn't have been any worse than my ski jump competition." Andrea encouraged him to continue.

"Well, you're probably right. I haven't heard anything that bad." Brent teased.

"Uh!" Andrea acted upset by gently swatting him on the bicep. His arm was calling her name; she just had to touch it - the real motivation behind the playful slap.

Brent continued, "At the end of my half-mile swim, I got a Charlie horse in my calf. Then, I couldn't find my bike when transitioning from my swim. Though I left the water before most of the athletes, they all passed me when they saw their bikes quickly.

"That is so awful." Andrea's compassion warmed Brent's heart.

"Oh, it gets better." Brent continued. "My calf cleared up, but about three-quarters of the way into the biking portion, my hamstring seized up on me. I had to get off my bike, rub it out a little, and then high-tail it to make sure I wasn't the last one transitioning into the five-kilometer run part of the event.

"Did your leg give you any more problems?" Andrea questioned genuinely.

"Yeah, I had to stretch out my calf and hamstring before I could even think about running. That cost me at least two minutes. I had lost ten looking for my bike. Overall, it took me twelve and a half minutes longer than my best training time."

Andrea saw an opportunity for contact again, so she ran her hand up and down his forearm, "I'm sorry, that must have been pretty discouraging."

Brent nodded and looked down at her hand on his arm. She started sliding it off, but Brent placed his hand on her, preventing her from taking it away.

Her heart picked up speed. A burning sensation shot up her neck. For a moment, they locked eyes. But thinking sensibly, Andrea looked away and pointed toward the road, "Do you mind watching the road? Not that anything worse could happen to me, but I don't want to see anything happen to you or Bruno."

"Of course, I am sorry."

Just as he pulled into her driveway, Andrea spoke. "You haven't shared anything about your family. Do you have brothers or sisters? Do your parents live around here?"

A nervous expression filled Brent's face. He ran his fingers through his hair and then along the stubble on his jaw. She noticed that he did those two movements when he got anxious. In an attempt to soften the moment, Andrea assured him she understood. "Families are tough, no pressure from me to share ... right this second." Her heart melted when Brent smiled at her, releasing air he must have held in for a while.

"Let's get inside first, then we can talk." Andrea nodded, hoping to encourage him. He put the truck in park and jumped out to get her chair.

Andrea grinned inwardly, realizing Brent would finally tell her why he had run out the night before. If she was lucky, he might also explain why he had frozen when she asked him about his family in the truck. They had come a long way from their phone conversations, arguing whether Andrea could zip line at his establishment.

Brent and Joe had walked ahead to open the door for her. He'd distracted her all day with his irresistible smell - spicy and clean. With every passing minute, Brent's lips were calling her name. She'd never been kissed the way he kissed her. In fact, his kisses were addictive. As excited as she was to hear about his family, she hoped there was time for more kisses.

Inside, Andrea gave Brent and Joe a full tour. Until now, Donna was the only person besides the contractor and crew who had seen the entire house. The big, spacious living room was the central hub of her home. A sliding glass door on the backside of the living room led to a deck where a ramp traversed toward the in-ground pool. "Was it hard getting used to the electric chair?" Joe asked as he pointed toward Andrea's only access to her pool.

"No. I had this house built especially for me after her accident, so the installers worked with me to make sure the accommodations were a match."

"Now that's what I'm talking about," Brent said, shifting the conversation to the hot tub.

Andrea felt her cheeks warm. She evoked an image of her and Brent finishing off a date, soaking together. Her daydream was cut short when Brent hurried the tour along.

They moved back through the living room and entered the spacious kitchen through a connecting, open doorway. Brent loved this room as much as he had the other night. The open window separating the kitchen and living room with barstools pushed underneath allowed an open concept. The countertops were smooth marble. In addition to many cupboards, there was a gigantic pantry big enough for Andrea to wheel her chair into and even turn around if she had to when leaving. A door to the right of the pantry led to a mudroom, which connected to a two-car garage.

Returning to the living room, she pointed down the hall, "The room on the left is the exercise room; the one on

the right is the bathroom. The other three doors are bedrooms."

"This place is huge," Joe blurted out, feeling a little
self-conscious after Andrea showed no emotion on her face.
Not wanting to offend her further, Joe sidled up to Donna,
who smiled at him and placed her arm around his waist.

"Thank you," the corner of Andrea's lip curled up.

"I just mean, I think it's great - especially an exercise
room. Joe admitted.

"You're welcome to go explore." Andrea pointed toward
the hall with her palm up in the most inviting way.

Joe grabbed Donna's hand and hurried to investigate the
room. This left Andrea and Brent alone. She invited him to
sit on the couch.

"Do you want help?" Brent stepped forward, offering to lift
Andrea on the couch.

"No, thank you. I do this all the time. I can't get in
your truck because it's so high off the ground." Andrea
explained.

Brent grinned.

"What?"

"I was making a mental note always to buy a truck high
off the ground," Brent said as he wagged his eyebrows at her.

The mere thought of Brent holding her in his arms made
her want to take his truck everywhere.

"Where'd all your DVDs go?" Brent asked with a sly smile
on his face.

Andrea played along, "I put all of them away except for
Aquaman." When Brent groaned, she knew that was the

confession he was looking for. "Just kidding. Why is that so important for you to know?"

"Just gauging the competition."

If Andrea had water in her mouth, it would have been sprayed across the room when she let out the biggest belly laugh of her existence. "You've got to be kidding me! That's the funniest thing I've ever heard." Andrea lowered her head, focusing on her hands that gently rubbed her athletic shorts between her thumb and forefinger.

"You know there's no contest, right?"

Brent scooted closer to Andrea. Her heart raced as he lifted her chin, forcing her to look at him. "Meaning?"

"I've got someone better than Aquaman sitting beside me."

"You are beautiful. The man you choose to finally let in will be luckier than a man who wins the lottery." Brent wrapped his other hand around her waist and drew her closer. She could see Brent's chest dramatically rising and falling. His gaze left her eyes and hovered over her mouth. Then, he dipped his head, letting his lips linger over hers. Andrea surprised him when she snaked her arms up around his neck, pulling him closer to her, and as their lips barely brushed each other, they heard the exercise door burst open. Brent jumped to the opposite sides of the couch as if they were teenagers and one of their parents just busted them in the act of kissing.

About that time, Bruno came barreling through his doggy door. He went right over to Brent and sniffed all around him. Brent gently rubbed the top of his head. Bruno sat back on his hind legs.

"You continue to pass the test," Donna smiled. "Bruno seems to like you, Brent," Donna explained how many times she had seen Bruno refuse to let people in the house that he didn't care for. While Donna shared the story in detail, Andrea plopped back in her chair and excused herself to the kitchen.

Oh, my lanta! Andrea saw it in Brent's eyes: desire for her. At least she told herself his desire was for her. She opened the freezer drawer and dipped her head to let the cold air smack her face.

As Andrea gathered the glasses, wine, and cheese, she placed them on a specially made table with wheels she'd had custom-made. When she heard them laughing, she knew that Donna got to the part when Bruno ripped a chunk of Dylan's pants off. Dylan was a friend of a friend who really turned out to be a jerk. He'd crossed the threshold, and Bruno didn't appreciate the intrusion. Andrea was so grateful for her buddy. She didn't need to learn the hard way when it came to people. He let her know who was good and who wasn't. According to Bruno, Brent was one of the good ones. Her heart skipped a beat, thinking about what might mean for them.

Brent took two long strides toward Andrea to contin-ue pushing the table toward the couch. Brent intentional-ly grazed her hand, locking eyes with her. Andrea's body shuttered with electricity at his simple touch. He must have stood there too long because Joe's question broke their gaze.

"Are you going to wheel that over here, or should I help you." Joe teased.

"Yeah, yeah," Brent grumbled, making Andrea giggle.

After wheeling the table between the loveseat, where Joe and Donna were, and the couch, Brent sat next to Andrea, who had just hoisted herself from her chair to the black leather couch. Their thighs gently skimmed each other as he leaned back, resting his broad shoulders on the back of the sofa.

The couples played Catch Phrase. Donna had gotten the game from the closet and explained the rules. "This is a handheld, fast-moving team game where the team member with the device gives clues to the remaining team members to guess the word on the screen. Joe and Donna protested at how competitive both Andrea and Brent were and wanted to play a different game. "Aw, just because we paid attention in school and can describe things better than you, it's not our fault," Brent used his best baby voice to goad Joe.

Brent raised his palm to Andrea, who slapped him with a high-five - another victory. The couple made a good team. Although, it had been clear that some of the points they earned came from Divine intervention. Based on the clues they gave, the other person couldn't have guessed the word, but somehow they did.

"It wouldn't have mattered what we played," Donna began. "Andrea would be competitive over Go Fish!" Everyone laughed, even Andrea. She knew the truth when she heard it. Donna put the game back in its box after Brent and Andrea won for the third time.

Andrea hopped back into her chair and wheeled toward the hall closet with Donna. "Thank you for getting that put away for me?" Andrea tugged Donna's hand, bringing her friend's ear toward Andrea's whispering mouth, "When are you and Joe leaving? Brent said we'd talk tonight. I don't want to give him any excuses to avoid a conversation?"

Donna whispered back, "Gotcha, consider us gone."

Meanwhile, Brent must have given Joe the same spiel based on the look shared between the two men when the ladies entered the living room. Joe, being Joe, plopped on the loveseat and rested his palms behind his head.

"Please go. I will lose my nerve if I have to wait any longer. After hearing my story, I need to see if Andrea wants to be with me. If not, I don't want to fall any further for her if she's going to ditch me." Brent pleaded with his friend to leave.

"That's not going to happen. Donna and I will be at your wedding. I see it very clearly." Joe whispered loudly, "She is too kind to ditch you."

"Shh shh." Brent jumped from the loveseat. He pulled Joe to his feet with a fist full of his buddy's shirt. Andrea laughed at Joe's dramatic acting.

Donna stood next to Joe, checking the non-existent watch on her wrist, "I think it's time to go home." Joe mimicked her when Donna gave him a slight jab to the shoulder. He jolted and announced, "I guess it's time to go. Thank you, Andrea ... Brent, I'll talk to you later."

Chapter 16

♥

Once alone, Brent stood and only took two strides before reaching Andrea's side. He snatched her up smoothly and gently placed her on the couch. When he sat next to her, their shoulders and legs connected. Being this close to Andrea sent flamethrowers shooting through Brent's body. He started sweating, anticipating sharing his past with her.

Andrea brought her wine glass to her lips. She must have sensed his gaze. "What?" she asked, resting her glass on her knee.

"Nothing, I'm sorry for staring." Brent didn't want to admit that he wished to be that glass. To touch her lips for a moment might squelch the fire burning in his chest. Brent shifted his body toward Andrea, bending his leg to parallel her thigh. Trying to relax, he rested his head on his hand, crooked on the back of the couch.

Andrea traced circles on her thigh. "So, are you ready to share whatever is on your mind?"

Brent shoved his hand through his hair. His heart raced, and the life-sized pit grew more prominent in his gut.

When he said nothing, Andrea said, "You know I was supposed to go skydiving, but I had to cancel."

Brent was surprised at the change of topic but appreciated it. He sent a silent thank you to God, as her skydiving story would lead him to share the story of Cherie. "Me too. When?"

"Right after my accident," Andrea admitted with regret. "I've looked into it again. There is a place in New Hampshire where I can tandem jump, even as a person with paraplegia. I think that might be my next adventure." her quest to enjoy life was as sexy to Brent as it was irritating. "Maybe you'd want to come with me?"

Warmth radiated through his body. Andrea was including him in future activities. Would she still want him around after he told her about Samantha? Hopefully.

First, he had to admit his previous failure to save his sister. If Andrea would rather throw him out of the plane without a parachute, well, he'd have his answer.

"I was supposed to go with Cherie," Brent raised his eyebrows and tilted his head slightly, wondering if Andrea would connect the name Cherie to the girl outside Guido's. She did. "We had been dating for a while. In retrospect, I can see now that she was faking her feelings - she didn't like me or anything we did. She wasn't an outdoors person...at all, but she faked it well."

Andrea's eyes never left him.

"Anyway, she broke up with me the day we were scheduled to skydive. I told Joe to go with another buddy of ours, so I still haven't been in a long time."

Brent stared at his lap.

"My first sky-diving experience was supposed to happen three and a half years ago, but everyone bailed on me then, so that's when I hiked Knife's Edge instead."

"By yourself?" Brent seemed astonished.

"Kyle was technically on the mountain or in the parking lot, I'm not sure. All I know is that he wasn't with me when it counted. But, yeah, I always hiked by myself because either a friend chickened out or Kyle changed his plans."

If Brent ever got his hands on Kyle, he'd be happy to smack some sense into that guy. How could he treat Andrea that way?

She shared her last experience hiking there. Brent extended his arm, then crooked it again on the back of the couch and rested his head back in his hand, urging her to continue with the story. He genuinely loved hearing Andrea talk but knew his time needed to come soon.

"I lost my footing and dangled on the edge before I could get one of my feet securely sandwiched between two rocks. I had tried to pull myself up but slipped again. If Kyle had been watching out for me, getting back up might have been easier, but he wasn't. He never had."

"I'm so sorry. How'd you get back to the top?"

"Another hiker. You probably heard the story of a seventeen-year-old girl who died when she lost her footing and her twenty-one-year-old brother grabbed her wrist but couldn't hang on. She slipped out of his hands and fell to her death. The newspapers held him accountable, but they were wrong."

"How do you know?" Brent asked, starting to sweat as his heart pounded against his ribs.

"Because I don't believe in accidents. God allows everything that happens to us. If He doesn't want it to happen, it won't. God would have allowed that brother to save his sister if He wanted to. Besides, that girl saved my life." Andrea declared.

Leaning upright, Brent asked, "How?"

Andrea hopped into her chair and asked Brent to follow her down the hall. When his eyes landed on a picture of Andrea and a young woman, Brent lost his breath. That pit in his stomach was now lodged in his throat. Suffocation. Write that on his tombstone as his cause of death. He couldn't believe the connection. There, staring back at him on Andrea's wall, adorned his first best friend. The one he wrestled with to help build her muscles and abilities. The one who followed him around, wanting to do everything he did... Tears pooled in his sockets.

"Are you okay, Brent?" Andrea asked when he didn't say anything. She yanked his arm down toward her, putting her hands on his shoulders. "What's wrong?" she asked, concerned echoed through the narrower space.

"Th-tha-that's my sister," Brent stammered out.

"Seriously?" Andrea said wide-eyed.

"Maybe we should go back to the couch," Brent squeezed his eyes shut as he pushed Andrea, hoping to stifle his emotions.

"Thank you for not running out again. You can trust me." Andrea's soft voice pierced Brent's thoughts as she hoisted herself onto the couch. Immediately, Andrea placed her hand on Brent's back.

Brent placed both of his elbows on his knees, cradling his head. Andrea gently dropped her hand from his upper arm and rested it on her lap. He sat up and turned his body toward Andrea. Gently, he ran his thumb up and down her forearm. "That was me."

Andrea searched Brent's eyes at first. He knew the moment she understood. Shock filled her eyes as they pooled with liquid. "You were the twenty-one-year-old brother?" her voice barely above a whisper.

A single tear fell down her cheek. She tried wiping it away quickly, but Brent beat her. His thumb gently brushed the tear off her cheekbone. "Oh, Brent ... I am so sorry you endured such a horrific event." Andrea wrapped her small hands around the outside of Brent's even though she couldn't cover them. "I've never believed anything the papers reported. That was a tragic accident. It had nothing to do with your ability to protect and save our sister or anyone else."

"Samantha." Brent choked out, moments away from tears himself.

"What a beautiful name. You are not responsible for Samantha's death." Andrea felt his shoulder tense, so she placed her hands on his shoulders and gently messaged them. "I truly believe everything happens for a reason. We will not know the reason for most things, but we have to have faith that it happened the way our sovereign God wanted it to, and He'll give us whatever we need to get through it *If* we ask Him."

Realizing that Andrea did not find him repulsive made him desire her even more than he already did. Andrea's warm hug comforted Brent and made him hot all over again. His body rejected the emptiness when she pushed back from their embrace. Man, he found Andrea so darn thrilling that he needed to make sure he wasn't alone in his desire, "Now that you know, are you still interested in exploring this new relationship between us?"

"Of course!" Genuinely confused, Andrea asked, "Why would your tragedy dissuade me from getting close to you?"

"Because I couldn't save Samantha. I figured I wouldn't be able to save or protect you. Every woman wants a man who can protect her, right?"

"Please!" Andrea pushed out a cheerful breath. "I already told you that I didn't believe the newspapers. Even if I had, I've had the pleasure of being in your arms." A slow smile stretched across his face as she gripped his biceps. "I felt pretty secure, so I'll take my chances." Andrea's coy smile set Brent's heart off like a rocket.

Brent leaned closer to tuck a loose tendril behind Andrea's ear. He rested his forehead on hers. His deep, husky voice whispered, "Andrea, you are so special. Thank you for not hating me after hearing that."

They were so close. Brent cradled her face, his hands slowly turned her toward him. His heart raced as he stared at her mouth, admiring her pouty lips. Then he pulled his eyes back to her eyes. He slowly bent his head toward Andrea's and covered her mouth with his. When she opened her mouth to kiss him back, he deepened the kiss, placing his hand at the nape of her neck and fisting her hair through his fingers. He interlaced his other fingers with Andrea's, resting their connected hands on her lap. He pulled away, resting his forehead against hers, trying to catch his breath. Her sweet fragrance stained his nostrils.

Brent didn't want to ruin this moment but needed to tell her about his parents. "There's a bit more," he whispered. "It's not as bad, in my opinion, so do you promise to kiss me again after I tell you." His lips curled into a feigned smile.

She mimicked him. "That depends on what you have to say, Mr. Smith." Andrea chaffed.

"After the accident, I pushed everyone away, even Joe, but he refused to go away." Brent grinned. "I was very selfish, only thinking about how I felt. One day, I arrived at my parent's house, and my dad had all the digital photo albums on his computer screen. He kept bringing up picture after picture of Samatha and different ones of us together."

He paused. The warmth of Andrea's hand on his encouraged him to keep going.

"Well, I snapped. We yelled; my mom tried to stop us. Before I stormed out of their house, he told me not to come back until I could accept Samantha's death and move on. A few months later, my mom texted me that they were moving to the Florida Keys. That was Samantha's favorite spot we vacationed." Brent let out a big burst of air, allowing his lungs to function properly.

Andrea sat silently for a long time. Brent searched her eyes for a response. "Wow. I don't know exactly what to say." Andrea's distressed look worried Brent.

He grabbed her hand and urged her, "Please just tell me."

"Okay, well, let me preface this with: I can't imagine how you feel because I haven't lived the last few years feeling responsible for a family member's death. Also, I have no clue what my relationship would have been like with my parents for the last eighteen months if they had survived to deal with me in this situation," she said, pointing at her chair.

Brent loved Andrea's kindness and thoughtfulness but didn't want any more disclaimers. He just wanted to know what she thought. "Give it to me straight."

"I think I feel bad for you and your parents. You all lost so much on that mountain. Now you've lost each other un-necessarily. Your way to grieve was isolating yourself; your dad's way to grieve was relishing in pictures of Samantha. You should have given each other the time and space to grieve how you needed." Andrea rubbed her hands up and down Brent's shoulder and bicep closest to her, trying to comfort him.

Brent wrapped his hand around Andrea's. Her soft, smooth hand fit perfectly in his palm. "I know you're right. Thank you. It's been so long, I wonder if my dad will even want to see me."

"Do you want to see your parents?" Andrea questioned.

"Yeah, I miss them a lot," Brent admitted. "I need to call them, huh?"

Andrea grinned, giving him his answer. "Thank you, Andrea."

"For what?"

"For caring." Brent gazed at her longingly. "Now, what about that kiss?" Brent rubbed his thumb up and down her forearm. When she shivered, he pulled her onto his lap and ran the tip of his nose along her jawline down her neck, stopping just above her collarbone. She always smelled like the ocean. He would gladly let her swallow him up.

"I'll kiss you under one condition." Andrea ran her painted fingernail over his lips, down his jawline, and tapped his pectoral muscles for emphasis. "You have to call your parents and reunite with them. They lost their daughter. It's not fair that they lost their son too."

Steady. My heart is going to explode. I knew it, I said to myself. This woman is the one for me. She cared about his relationship with his parents. Before he could tell her the situation, she'd already discredited the reporters, as Joe had already told him to do. Andrea leaned closer to Brent, who closed his eyes in anticipation. At the last moment, she lightly kissed Brent's cheek, "Promise me you'll call them." Andrea demanded in a low whisper.

Brent opened his mouth to answer, yet nothing came out. It's like he had a ball lodged in his throat, preventing him from talking. He needed to promise Andrea and get out of here before he disappointed his mom even more by acting on his impure thoughts, "P-Pr. I promise." Brent stammered out.

"Good." Andrea pressed her lips to Brent's. The instant their lips met, Brent took complete control, deepening the kiss. He ran his hands up and down her back in a tender, soft, caressing way, though he kissed her with such pent-up passion a body-jolting alarm sounded in his head: *STOP!*

Breaking for air, Brent hugged her. "We need to stop so I can stay in God's good grace." He kissed her cheek and checked if she needed any help before he left, which she declined. "Good night, Andie."

Andrea's beaming smile filled the room. "Goodnight, Brent."

He kissed the top of her head, locked her door, and shut it securely.

Brent stuck his phone into the mount hanging from his windshield and laughed, overjoyed. Relief flooded his body, knowing Andrea knew the truth and didn't hate him. At that moment, he knew he was in love with Andrea.

Chapter 17

♥

"Ms. Williams, this is Dr. Crawford's office."

Andrea gripped the phone, anticipating the receptionist's following words.

"One of our patients needed to post-pone surgery, so you're next on the list. Are you prepared to have surgery this coming Thursday?"

"Uh. Um. Yeah." Andrea stammered. "How should I prepare?"

The woman's voice on the other end of the phone sounded more like white noise or Charlie Brown's teacher as Andrea fervently wrote down what she needed to do in the next two days.

"Do you have any questions?" The out-of-breath woman asked.

"None right now, but that might change in twenty-four hours." Andrea let out a jagged breath.

"Not a problem. If you have any questions, please call back. Otherwise, Dr. Crawford will see you bright and early Thursday morning. Have a great day."

"You, too. Bye." Andrea stared at the phone as it disconnected. Then, her adrenaline kicked in. She tapped on Donna's contact. Her friend answered on the second ring. Andrea rambled off all the new information she just received.

"Wait. You're having surgery like the day after tomorrow?"

"Yeah. Will you take me? I need to be there at six-thirty."

The silence on the other end of the phone felt like a weight sinking in her stomach. "Donna."

"I told the guys I'd work at the store because they were going to climb Knife's Edge."

"Seriously?" disappointment bubbled up in Andrea.

"It's the anniversary of his sister's death; he brings her flowers every year," Donna explained.

Andrea felt like a heel. *Of course, he'd do something sweet like that.* "Oh, man. Okay. That's not a problem. I can have an Uber bring me."

"Can we talk later? I have to finish this order."

"Sure thing. Talk soon. Bye." Andrea disconnected. She felt awful for jumping to conclusions, but she did wonder why Brent hadn't told her he was going. Did he feel guilty climbing the mountain when he knew Andrea wanted to and couldn't? She couldn't worry about that right now. She needed to focus on her surgery - the potential of walking again.

Excitement ran through her veins. She reread her notes.

- *Arrive at 6:30*

- *Where loose bagging clothes*

- *Bring 2 sets of clothes; discharge will depend on my progress*

- *PT scheduled to start Saturday; all set up; coming to the house*

- *PT daily until the therapist changes frequency.*

- *Nothing to eat after 7 PM Wednesday; water only*

- *No water after 2:30 AM*

- *Need a person to drop me off and pick me up*

Andrea spent the rest of her day at the rock climbing gym. Dan let her start on the second intermediate wall she ended on her last visit. She rang the bell in under four minutes.

"That's great," Dan said as he prepared for the next wall. "How long is the recovery?"

"That depends on my body and how well I listen to the therapist. They start working my legs immediately, so I hope it's a quick turnaround time."

Dan tested the strap to ensure it was secure around Andrea and her chair. "Ready?"

"Let's go." Andrea hoisted herself on the two bottom jugs and quickly swung to the right, securing her forearm on the nearest jug.

Dan continued to holler out directives that she followed successfully and crushed the third intermediate wall under her four-minute mark.

Andrea wrapped up her final intermediate wall as the sun closed its eyes to the beautiful autumn day. "Maybe I can try the advance wall before my surgery."

"Don't overdo it. Maybe you won't be in your chair the next time you climb." Dan unwrapped up the strap as he talked.

"*I* won't be *my* chair for much longer." Andrea's eyes and voice beamed.

"Hey, if I don't see you before your surgery, Good luck. You're very strong, so if anyone will heal before the standard time frame, it'll be you."

"Thanks for all your help today, Dan."

When Andrea made it to her car, she had eight missed texts: two from Brent and six from Donna. She clicked on Brent's banner first.

Brent: Hey, How's your day going?

He'd sent it at ten o'clock this morning. That was the time she started her first climb. The following text came in at noon.

Brent: Are you available for lunch? If not, how about dinner?

She felt bad. Brent probably thought she was ignoring him when, in reality, she didn't have her phone. She would text him after she saw all of Donna's texts.

Donna: I told the guys about your surgery. They will ask one of the ropes supervisors to cover the store so I can take you. Are you nervous?

Donna: Where are you?

This text had come in at eleven-thirty, only an hour and a half after her first one.

Donna: This isn't funny. Where are you?

Surprisingly, Donna waited almost two hours before sending this text.

Donna: If you don't respond in five minutes, I am calling the police and reporting a missing person.

Her next text came twelve minutes later, so she hadn't called the police.

Donna: I'd like to know where you are. Why aren't you responding?

Donna: You're not funny. Where are you? Andrea, please call me. The guys are concerned now, too.

Andrea chuckled at her friend. She knew Donna wouldn't call the police, but she felt terrible when she *heard* the worry in her text. Now she got the guys involved.

Her first call was to Donna. The phone hadn't finished the first ring before she answered. "Andrea, where have you been?

"I was at the rock climbing gym. I got through all the intermediate walls—"

"—You could have called or texted before now. We've been worried all day. You could have fallen or something. We didn't have a clue where you were." Donna cut Andrea off to express her displeasure.

Andrea refrained from rolling her eyes. "Okay, Mom. Next time, I'll be sure to text you before I leave the house."

"No need to be snarky. I was really worried about you."

"Thank you, I appreciate that, but are you going to feel the same way once I can walk again, or are you just concerned because I'm in a chair?"

It was a valid question. Andrea didn't want to be a burden on anyone, but she wanted everyone's concern for her to be authentic and not because she was disabled.

"I don't care how you get around. I still worry about you and will continue until the day I die."

Andrea apologized again. This time, Donna accepted it.

Once they hung up, Andrea texted Brent.

Andrea: Sorry. I was rock climbing all day. It's late now, but we could do dinner tomorrow.

Three dots appeared on the bottom left.

Brent: It's not too late. I could bring dinner to you if that's not too pushy.

Giddiness took over. Andrea was glad she texted before leaving the parking lot, but now she'd have to hurry home before Brent arrived.

Andrea: I'm still in the parking lot. I won't be home and ready for an hour.

Brent: I know it only takes twenty minutes to get to your home from the gym. I'm missing forty minutes somewhere.

Andrea: I have to get ready.

Brent: You're gorgeous. You can't improve perfection.

Aw, that's sweet but not true.

Andrea: Thou shall not lie. *smile emoji*

Brent: I'll see you in about an hour *wink emoji*

It turned out that Andrea didn't need an hour after all. After taking her shower and throwing on some leggings and an oversized tee shirt, the doorbell rang. She wheeled to the living room, where she heard Bruno barking aggressively.

Then, a familiar, unwelcomed voice from the past filled the room.

"Andrea. Come get your dog."

For a brief moment, she froze in the middle of the living room. "Bruno, come here." Bruno trotted next to Andrea's chair, turned, and sat on his hind legs, keeping his eyes fixed on the intruder before him.

For what seemed like an eternity, Andrea just stared at the man at the front door. No, he wasn't a man, but rather a coward who ran out on her because she couldn't walk.

"Kyle, what are you doing here?" Andrea finally found her voice. He still had stalky, muscular arms and legs, but he didn't look as attractive to her anymore. Her mom had always told her that the most attractive man on the outside could be the ugliest, while a less physically attractive person could be the most handsome. Then there were people like Brent who were physically irresistible, fun, thoughtful, and sweet.

"Can I come in, Andrea? I want to talk." Kyle sheepishly put one foot in front of the other.

Andrea left the door half-open so Kyle would get the hint that he couldn't stay long. "I guess so?" She hoped her coldness was well noted.

"There's my girl - all sassy—"

"—I am not your girl," Andrea cut him off. "Remember you dropped me the minute I couldn't walk." Andrea folded her arms across her chest. Her tone was even but deep to ensure Kyle didn't think she still had feelings for him.

She most definitely did not! A little peace rained over Andrea when Bruno looked at her as if to ask *do you want me to escort him out of here?*

"Andie don't—"

"—You can't call me that. Only my friends call me that. You no longer fit into that category." She heard the irritation in her voice. *So much for staying calm.*

Kyle snorted. "What did you expect? I am not good at taking care of someone. You needed around-the-clock care, and that's not me."

"Yet, here I am, living alone." Bruno whimpered. "Living with Bruno," she corrected. "And doing just fine."

Kyle moved closer. Bruno growled. Andrea smiled when he returned to his spot. "I see that." The sultry tone he used as he looked her up and down made her want to hurl. "I heard you won a wheelchair race, and you're rock climbing like a pro."

"How do you know that?"

"It's all over the internet, Andrea." Kyle thought his statement explained everything when it told her nothing.

"I'm not following."

Kyle pulled out his phone, pulled up the video, handed it to her, and stepped back to his spot when Bruno raised a paw like he was about to invade the man's space.

Shock filled Andrea when her picture appeared in the video. She pressed the volume button to hear a woman's voice explaining how an accident had taken her parents and her ability to walk and then her boyfriend. Then she tried to make Andrea sound like a comeback kid. She hadn't thought of herself like that. She just tried to live life doing the things she liked.

When the reporter appeared in a square at the bottom of the video, anger rose in Andrea. Brent's old girlfriend. *Did he tell her about all about me the day he slipped and said I was his girlfriend?* She didn't finish the video. "Here. What was the point in showing me this? Why are you here?"

"I'd like to give us another try. You can get around well and do the things we loved doing together, so why not try again? When Andrea hadn't responded, Kyle continued. "If there's something you can't do, I will just do it with the guys."

Andrea exhaled loudly.

Just then, Kyle lowered himself to one knee. *Is he seriously proposing?*

"I got scared, but I'm not anymore. I want you in my life. Will you—"

Andrea laughed, putting an abrupt stop to his question, "You're seriously not going to ask me to marry you, are you?"

"I was, but I guess your laughter is my answer." Kyle stood up and rubbed his hand through his hair. That reminded Andrea of Brent.

"You realize your arrogance and selfishness will keep you from any meaningful relationship. I think it's time you should go. I have plans tonight that I don't want to be late for."

"Who are your friends, Jack, Janet, and Chrissy," Kyle pointed toward the sitcom cover on her table.

"Leave... now!"

"I'm sorry I hurt you," Kyle sneered.

Andrea chuckled to herself at his narcissist's attitude. "You didn't hurt me. You did me a favor. I should say thank you for saving me a lot of wasted time and frustration." Andrea gave Kyle a placated smile. She wasn't trying to be mean. "I wish you the best for your life, Kyle."

"Whatever, Andrea. I never should have listened to my mom and proposed. You've been useless since your accident, and that won't change."

At that moment, Brent stormed through the partially opened door as a low growl emerged deep from within Bruno.

"Who are you?" Kyle barely had time to ask before Brent had the guy by the shirt against Andrea's wall. Kyle looked over Brent's shoulder. Bruno stood on all fours right behind Brent, like the best backup partner ever.

"You worthless twit. Don't you ever talk to my girlfriend like that again! If you ever show your face around her again, Bruno and I will rearrange it for you. Do we understand each other?"

"Y–Y–yeah." Kyle stammered out his whisper.

His feet dangled about a foot off the ground. His dilated pupils and chalk-white face assured Andrea that Kyle was scared. He should be. Her heart swooned for Brent, the way the muscles in his forearm bulged with his fists tightly gripping the front of Kyle's shirt.

"What, I didn't hear that?"

Bruno growled a little more, showing his fangs to Kyle.

"Yes. I understand." Kyle squealed out in a high-pitched voice.

Brent still didn't release him. "Apologize to my woman." When Kyle said nothing, Brent pulled him away from the wall and shoved his back against it. "Now."

"I'm sor-sorry, Andrea. I'll never bother you again."

"Better." Brent set Kyle on his feet. "Now, get out of here before I sick Bruno on you too."

Kyle shimmed around the open door, never taking his eyes off Bruno. He clutched the doorknob and closed it securely.

Brent was on his knees at Andrea's side. "Are you okay?"

Her emotions were running high. Yes, Brent had just demonstrated that he'd protect her. It was Oscar-worthy, but the video still had her mind racing.

"Thank you. That was a great way to show you can protect me." She smiled at him.

Brent kissed her temple. "Why was he here?"

She cleared her throat. "Apparently, to show me some video your old girlfriend made about me and to propose."

"What?!" Brent searched her face. She half appreciated the concerned look on his face; it looked like he didn't have a clue about a video yet, but he seemed to have some understanding of the overall topic.

"I thought you could shed some light on the subject for me." Andrea crossed her arms over her chest.

Brent reached for her hand. Bringing it to his lips, he planted firm kisses on the inside of her wrist and palm. "The day she came into the shop, she asked if I would give her access to you for a story. I told her she had to stay away from you. That's when I called you my girlfriend."

"I didn't watch the whole video. Is there more?" Andrea questioned.

He offered a feigned smile. "I'm not sure. All I know is that I told her I wouldn't work with her and that she needed to leave you alone. How she got any information to make a video is beyond me. It doesn't surprise me, but I didn't help it along." He let out a big breath. I will contact her and make her pull it ... somehow.

"No. It's okay. From what I saw, it wasn't anything negative. I'd rather forget about the whole thing."

Brent crossed his arm over his chest. "If that's what you want."

"Were you embarrassed of me?" Andrea dipped her head and pulled her hand back, wrapping it around her midsection.

"No. Of course not." Brent pulled her hand back and laced their fingers together. "I am so sorry you thought that. Brent tucked a strand of hair behind her ear and guided her head toward him. "If I were embarrassed by you, I wouldn't have gone to dinner, the beach, or anywhere else with you."

Andrea had struggled with self-image since the accident. Her thoughts had dehumanized her. Brent's sweet words should have quenched her need for further reassurance, but doubt was a funny thing. It stuck around like green on grass, only fading briefly during the off-season. Then, it came back stronger than ever in other seasons. For now, all she could do was take him at his word.

Sweat droplets formed at Brent's hairline. She'd only seen that one other time when he was nervous around her. It seemed odd to her that he'd feel that way now after they'd come so far. She hated to admit it, but he looked irresistible in this nervous state. *How is that even possible?*

"Are you okay, Brent?"

He rubbed his palm along his jaw, distracting her. All she could think about was how the texture of the short stubble would feel against her palm. *Whoa, settle down, girl.*

In an attempt to speak, Brent stumbled over his words and snapped his lips shut. "Let's try this again." He ran his fingers up and down her shoulder intimately. "Andrea, I am the opposite of embarrassed of you. I'm falling for you."

Chapter 18

♥

PATIENCE WAS ONE OF Brent's strong qualities, but not today. A big bundle of nerves, Brent paced the waiting room Thursday afternoon. He'd changed his plans and hiked Samantha's flowers up to her Wednesday so he could bring Andrea to her surgery. They couldn't believe it when he told his parents, but they would fly out and visit. *They probably suspected I was lying.*

He'd gotten Andrea to the hospital at six-thirty like they were supposed to, but her actual surgery didn't start until eight. It'd taken an hour and a half to prep her for the next seven hours, or so he thought.

The doctor said seven hours max. Brent watched as the minute hand struck the twelve. Five o'clock. It'd been nine hours, and he hadn't heard a word. Andrea gave the nurse her power of attorney paperwork during the pre-surgery, putting Donna in charge of decisions. She also signed paperwork allowing the nurses to provide all information to Brent; he just didn't have the power to make decisions.

When his phone rang, he answered it before the second ring finished. "Hey, Joe."

"How's everything going?"

Brent scoffed. "Heck, if I know. She's been in surgery for nine hours. I haven't been told a thing except that the doctor will talk to me when they are finished."

"I'm sure everything is fine. I just sent Donna over there. I'll head over when I get the all-clear from night security. Need anything?"

"Nah, I'm good. Thanks, Man."

It wasn't long after he hung up that the doctor emerged from the oversized *Do Not Enter* doors that they wheeled Andrea through too many hours ago. "Mr. Smith." Brent turned in mid-stride.

"Yes, how is Andrea?"

"She is in recovery. You should be able to see her when she wakes up. The surgery took a little longer than expected, but everything went well. No complications. I'll have the nurse come out to get you when you can join Andrea unless you have questions for me now."

"No, I'm good, Doctor. Thank you. Brent shook the older man's hand before the doctor disappeared behind the same massive doors he entered through moments ago.

Emotion suffocated Brent. His chest ached, thinking of how strong Andrea was to endure an evasive surgery for so many hours. He was fully invested in this woman. That scared him. *Lord, thank you so much for guiding those doctor's hands. I'm sorry if I annoyed you today with all my prayers. Please help me do whatever is necessary for her healing.*

"Brent." Donna came rushing into the waiting room. "Have you heard anything?"

He explained what the doctor said. He hated this waiting game, but at least he had a friend to wait with. When Joe got there, it would be even better.

"What's the plan for helping her during her recovery? Brent asked Donna.

"You know her. She will drive the physical therapist crazy but push herself with her exercises to make sure she heals quickly." Donna started to pace with Brent.

Brent chuckled. "Oh, I know that. Are you staying with her?"

"I hadn't planned on it." Donna shook her head. "You know how independent Andrea is; she'll never allow that."

Brent crossed his arms over his chest. "Do you think she'd let me stay on the couch or in one of those spare bedrooms?"

Donna burst out laughing. "You have a better chance of aliens landing at your doorstep than staying at Andrea's."

"I'd only be there to help her. Everything would be completely platonic."

Before Donna could say anything, a nurse brought them to see Andrea.

"It's okay, Andrea. I'll stay here with you tonight." Brent placed his hand over hers, engulfing her petite fingers.

Still groggy, Andrea retorted. "It's not okay. I still don't know why the surgery took longer than they said it would. I was told it was a day surgery, and now I have to stay here."

Thankfully, the doctor arrived and explained things to a worried Andrea.

"Since you've been in your state longer than our typical patient, we inserted a few more electrodes for good measure. The surgery couldn't have gone any better. I'll check in with you first thing tomorrow morning. If everything looks good, I'll send you home."

Andrea smiled. "Thank you, Doctor."

"When does her PT start?" Donna asked before the older gentleman left.

"They'll work with her first thing in the morning. Then the in-home therapist will show up on Saturday." Looking toward Andrea, "Tomorrow, you should receive a call confirming the time."

Once the doctor left, Brent moved closer to the head of Andrea's bed. He rubbed his thumb over her forehead. "Are you hungry or thirsty?"

"I could use a drink, thank you."

Brent retrieved the cup of water and held the straw to Andrea's lips. Thinking about that jerk, Kyle, who left Andrea when she needed help the most, made him want to hunt him down and punch him just for fun. He regretted not doing that when he had him up against the wall. Any help she needed was temporary. Brent vowed to be there for her every step of the way.

Andrea removed the straw. "Thank you."

"No problem. When you want more, let me know."

"Sure. Will you feed me grapes, too?" Andrea joked.

"Absolutely, Princess." Brent winked at her as he sent the cup down.

Andrea rolled her eyes. "I was kidding."

"I'm not."

Donna smiled at Andrea. "Whoa. Is it hot in here?"

Brent felt his cheeks warm when Donna pointed out the chemistry between him and Andrea. Thankfully, Joe came bursting into the room with flowers. *No. Flowers. Why hadn't I thought of that?*

"Here you go, Brent; I picked these up for you as you asked." Joe handed them off to Brent, who mouthed, *Thank you.*

Joe hurried over to Donna and kissed her on the cheek while Brent presented the flowers to Andrea.

"Thank you. They are beautiful."

"Just like you." Brent kissed Andrea on the forehead and laid the flowers on her table.

Joe turned his attention to Andrea. "How are you doing?"

"Great. I should be going home now."

"Can you feel anything?"

"Joe!" Donna and Brent snapped in unison. Donna back-handed his shoulder, too.

"It's okay." Andrea chuckled. "I can't. They drugged me up good. The nurse told me I'll know it when the meds wear off."

They ate dinner and chatted while Andrea slipped in and out of consciousness. When the nurse came in to let them know that visiting hours were over, she also had a pillow and blanket. "Don't keep the patient up, and you can stay." The older woman winked at Brent.

"Thank you."

Once Brent and Andrea were the only ones in the room, he brushed his thumb over her forehead and kissed the top of her head. He slid the chair closer to the side of her bed, situated his pillow, and leaned back, mesmerized by this woman sleeping less than a foot away from him. As he gazed hopelessly at Andrea, who stormed out of his park just about a month ago, he knew he'd do anything to make life easier for her and fun.

When she woke up the next morning, Brent had already been up, folded his blanket, and given that and his pillow to the nurse, making sure to thank her for all her help during the night with Andrea.

Last night, or early this morning, he wasn't sure; Andrea woke up screaming in pain. As much as his heart ached for her, her determination, strength, and positive attitude stood out to him and the nurse. Before she drifted back to sleep, she said, " I guess all this pain means the surgery was a success." Brent adored this woman.

"Hello, Sunshine. How are you this morning?" Brent stood by her bed, reaching out to take her hand. She welcomed it.

"Thank you for staying with me. I really appreciate you being here when I thought I would die." She chuckled, causing him to mimic the same sound, not surely not as sweet sounding as hers.

He kissed the back of her head. "It was my pleasure."

"I hate to ask you this ... you can say no if you want ... but I feel God is pushing me to ask you ..."

Brent smiled at her inability to say what was on her mind. He'd never seen this before. Her cheeks had a tinge of pink; this was endearing. "Ask me anything. Your wish is my command." He did a half-bow thing that made him feel ridiculous after the fact, but the smile on her face was worth it.

"Based on last night's episode, I think it might be a good idea if someone was with me for a few nights..." Brent's heart threatened to thump right out of his chest. *Is she going to ask me to stay and help her?*

"...would you stay in one of my spare bedrooms to help me?"

"Definitely." *Thank you, Lord. This is what love really feels like, huh?* Would Andrea accept his love?

Chapter 19

♥

Things with Brent were moving along quickly. She'd never thought she'd connect with anyone after her parents' death and Kyle left. It turned out that she connected with Brent in a way that she never could with Kyle. Everything with Kyle had been about their adventures. Brent had an active lifestyle, but there was more to him and their time together than that.

It'd been two weeks since Andrea's surgery. Brent had been by her side twenty-four-seven. During the day, Joe and Donna closed the shop for the winter. Then they visited at night. Tonight, Andrea made Brent go for a run with Joe. He'd admitted that he liked her gym and used that daily while she had physical therapy with Bob, but she needed some girl time with Donna as much as she assumed he needed his best friend.

"How are you feeling today?"

"Pretty good. Bob still has me doing ankle pumps. I have kept praying for patience since I couldn't move my ankles a week ago, and now I can, but I want to do more." Andrea grabbed her tablet. "Do you want to see?"

"Yeah." Donna stood beside Andrea, who was already stretched out on the couch.

Andrea selected a button on her tablet, commanding her brain to tell her spinal cord to move her ankles. When her ankles started moving slowly, Donna screeched. "That's amazing."

Just then, Andrea's default cellphone ringtone blared. "As Long as We've Got Each Other," the theme song to the eighties sitcom, "Growing Pains" jumped her.

Then another: "As long—"

And another: "As long as—"

And another: "As long as we—"

"What the heck?" Andrea said to the air in the room. "What could be that important?"

And another: "As long—" Normally, she let the short clip play in its entirety because she loved that theme song, but even Kirk Cameron would have thrown the phone across the room after that onslaught of texts.

By the time Andrea traded the tablet for her phone, the banner at the bottom read Brent five messages.

Brent: We ended up at the store. I noticed you were low on your emergency ice cream.

Brent: *image of Ben and Jerry's Chunky Monkey*

Brent: *image of Ben and Jerry's Phish Food*

Brent: *image of Ben and Jerry's Cherry Garcia*

Brent: *image of a pint of Twix ice cream*

Looking over her shoulder, Donna smiled. "For Brent to know about your ice cream obsession, you must be getting close."

Seeing Brent's strong forearm holding each ice cream flavor made him even more appealing than before. Especially the Twix pint. She'd just told him last night as they talked into the wee hours of the morning that she wanted to try it. *He really must have listened. Did he hear everything I said?*

"Earth to Andrea." Donna waved her hand in Andrea's face.

"What?"

"You're hooked on Brent." Donna cheered.

"Am not. Andrea muttered. Panic. That's what she felt. She couldn't be falling for Brent. Wasn't he just being a nice guy helping her out? The last thing she needed to do was mistake his decency for something more. "Just because a guy does something nice for a female doesn't mean he's in love with her."

He did tell me he was falling for me. Since he had yet to bring it up again, she didn't mention this to Donna. He could have had a moment of weakness when he said it.

"I wasn't talking about his feelings..." Donna searched her friend's eyes. "You like him, don't you?"

Andrea frowned. "It doesn't matter. I really believe he's just being a nice guy. No point in ruining that. He'll be a great friend." She wrapped a band that Bob had given her around the ball of her foot and gently pulled it toward her body.

Donna shook her head. "I think you should talk with him before you start assuming things. It's almost Christmas; anything can happen."

"I think you're a little early. Thanksgiving is still two weeks away, so Christmas is not on my mind yet. Besides, Brent is returning to work next week. We won't be around each other all day, every day, and he'll forget about me.

"Not a chance." Donna shook her head. "Besides, Joe and I only have a little to wrap up tomorrow, and they are closed for the winter."

One of the many things Andrea appreciated about Donna was her ability to deliver a message and then be silent to let the person think about what she said. It wasn't long after she finished stretching both feet that the guys arrived.

If she didn't know better, Brent had a twinkle in his eye when he smiled at her. She probably imagined it, but that's okay since it was a great look on him.

"We're going to get headed," Donna announced, pulling Joe up by the shirt as he tried to sit in the chair closest to the door.

"Alrighty then." Joe stood erect, waved to Andrea, and wished her a good night.

Speak. Say anything. After her conversation with Donna, Andrea now felt awkward. "Thank you for picking up ice cream. Which one did you get?"

Setting the bag on the table before her, he said, "I got them all." He handed her each pint, one by one. "Would you like to dig into one now?"

"Brent. I can't believe you got all of them. That was really sweet and thoughtful."

Straight-faced, he deadpanned, "Don't tell anyone I'm sweet. It'll ruin my image."

Andrea busted out laughing. "What image?"

Brent pulled out his shirt and rolled his shoulders back. "I'm the big, bad, tough guy who owns the best Adventure Park in the state."

Andrea rolled her eyes and let out a chuckle she couldn't contain. "Well, I'll call you sweet every chance you give me. If people are around, that's your fault."

"No one's around now." Brent slowly lowered his lips to hers and lingered there. His soft lips were like a fleece blanket warming her to her core. When he pulled back, he only moved half an inch. His breath moved a strand of her hair when he said, "I'll be back with some spoons."

If Andrea could have hopped, she would have put the Energizer Bunny to shame. This was the first time she could recall her cheekbones ached from smiling so big. *Is it possible Brent meant it when he said he was falling for her?*

Once he arrived with the spoons, he handed them to Andrea and lifted her legs. He promptly sat on the couch, resting her calves over his thighs. The intimacy of that movement warmed Andrea's heart.

"Which one would you like tonight," Brent asked.

"The Twix one, please." He handed it to her. "Thank you so much for listening to me last night. I was surprised when you sent me the picture of this one." She held up the pint he just handed her.

Brent tore off the lid of the Phish Food. "Of course, I listen to you."

They ate their ice cream in comfortable silence for the next few moments. Then, Brent followed Andrea's lead and put the lid on his ice cream. He brought their desserts to the freezer.

When he returned, Andrea let her nerves take over and started rambling about nothing to avoid letting Donna's thoughts take over and sharing her feelings with Brent.

He rubbed his hand over his neck and drew in a long breath.

"Am I keeping you from something more important?" Her playful tone clutched at his heart.

Brent produced a smile that reached his eyes, "On no, I'm just hoping I don't forget what I want to say by the time you get done."

"Be my guest," Andrea pinched her thumb and forefinger together and whisked them across her lips to show she would zip her lips.

"I don't want to be friends with you." Confusion filled Andrea's eyes, and she knew he recognized it as it slapped him in the face. "This is not going the way I planned." Brent clenched his jaw and rubbed a hand through his hair. "Look, you've made me feel alive the last couple of months."

"Better so far," Andrea encouraged him.

"I've realized that I ... I'd like to ... I've fallen for you!" Brent finally announced for a second time.

Andrea's pulse raced as Brent gazed into her eyes. *Had Donna somehow told him what they'd talked about? Lord, this has to be you, right?*

Breathe Girl. Heat rose in Andrea's cheeks. "You make me feel alive too." She dropped her eyes to where he'd taken up residency next to her on the couch. His eyes slowly moved up to her lips and stopped before he met her eyes again.

Brent cleared his throat and gently pinched her chin between his thumb and forefinger, guiding her head upward level with his. Without further hesitation, Brent lowered his mouth to hers and covered her lips gently at first. Andrea immediately melted into his chest. She placed both her hands there to steady herself.

Steady, yeah, right!

Brent's chiseled chest caused Andrea even more distraction. She let her arms drift gently down his broad shoulders, resting on his hulking biceps. Brent's fingers enveloped Andrea's hair at the nape of her neck while his other hand pressed on her hip, pressing her closer. A low moan escaped both of them as Brent deepened the kiss.

Pulling away to catch her breath, Andrea brushed her fingers over her puffy, almost numb lips, ensuring they were still there. Brent rested his forehead on Andrea's to catch their breath.

Brent swooped her onto his lap. "I'm hoping you'll be mine and all mine."

The idea of Brent being all hers set a flurry of pyrotechnics off in her chest. "Are you sure?"

"Yes," Brent placed his palm on her cheek and chuckled. "By the way, my parents will be here tomorrow," Brent revealed.

Andrea's head jerked away from his hand. "What? I thought they were coming for Thanksgiving." Panic flooded her chest.

"My mom is so excited to meet you. They wanted more time to visit," he explained as he rubbed his hand up her arm.

Brent's smile faded when Andrea uttered, "I can't meet your parents tomorrow!"

"Why?" Brent shrugged.

"What if your mom doesn't like me?" Andrea worried aloud.

"She already loves you," Brent admitted.

"How is that possible?" Andrea raised her eyebrows and crossed her arms over her chest, acting upset, but she wasn't.

Brent smiled as he rubbed his hand down one side of his face, "I may have told her how great you are already. And please don't be mad, but I told her how Samantha saved you. I know it wasn't my story to tell, but ..."

"It's okay, she's your sister." Andrea rubbed her hand through Brent's silky hair. "I don't know how I feel about meeting your parents, especially like this. Andrea pointed toward her legs.

"Please don't worry." Brent kissed her cheek. "You are perfect."

They spent the rest of the night watching Andrea's eighties sitcoms, laughing and cuddling on the couch. If anyone had told her a year ago that she'd be enjoying her sitcoms with a handsome man, she would have told them they were crazy.

Once he helped her to bed, she did her stretches again and handed him her band. He softly kissed her head. "Good night, Andrea."

"Good night, Brent."

Andrea stared at the ceiling for a long while, nervous about meeting Brent's parents the next day. Before she drifted off to sleep, she wondered if Brent thought meeting his parents was as big a deal as she did.

Chapter 20

♥

Brent's rapid blinking helped block out the bright morning sun streaming through the window. It had snowed overnight, so the reflection made it even more bright.

He threw the covers off his legs and threw on some athletic shorts and a muscle shirt. He'd be lying if he said having access to Andrea's gym wasn't convenient. He strapped on his smartwatch and laced up his gym shoes.

When he opened the door, he heard Andrea and Bob talking. She gave him a shy smile as he walked into the room. They were working on her ankle stretches, and she didn't seem impressed.

"Good morning. How's the therapy going?" Brent eyed Bob briefly but settled on Andrea.

"I'd be doing much better if the tablet didn't give me a hard time." Andrea huffed.

Brent placed his hand on her shoulder. Everything takes time. You'll get there." Focusing on Bob, he asked, "Do I have a green light for what we discussed?"

"Yeah. I'll still be here at seven-thirty, so you must go early. It will be interesting to see how her body responds."

"Could you two stop talking about me like I'm not in the room? Where are we going?" She pulled back on the band a little further this time as she looked at Brent expectantly.

Brent adored Andrea's beautiful face. "I thought we could go swimming tomorrow like you asked the other day. We'd have to leave at five-thirty to get there, swim, and return for Bob."

"If that's what it takes, I'll be ready. Thank you."

"For what?" Brent asked, full of smiles.

Andrea cupped the side of Brent's face, feeling a day's worth of stubble beneath her palm. "You made something happen for me and didn't argue about my potential inability."

Brent moved his head closer to Andrea's. "Funny how that works. You didn't argue with me about doing it yourself."

She opened her mouth slightly to say something, but Brent surprised her by capturing her lips with his before he took off for the exercise room.

He heard Bob give her orders for the next exercise. "Grab your walker." Brent was impressed with Andrea. He didn't hear her complain about the hard word once. He may have moaned and groaned because her body was stiff and it was hard work, but she always did one more rep beyond what Bob asked.

It had been over a week since his parents arrived. As he predicted, his parents loved Andrea, but especially his mom. As Brent began his circuit of squats, shoulder presses, a deadlift, and a bicep curl, he recalled his mother's tears when he saw the picture of Samantha on Andrea's wall. Almost instantly, she'd wanted Andrea to tell her the story, as she proceeded to cry even more.

His dad enjoyed the story, too, but he'd told Brent how nice it was to have a strong woman by his side. "I know, Mom's great."

"I'm not talking about Mom and I." His dad shook his head. "When I saw Andrea on the stationary bike and witnessed her tears of frustration quickly turn into determination ... that's a strong woman you have."

"Dad, I'm sorry about yelling at you."

"It's water under the bridge. We both had to give each other grace, and we didn't. Here's to the future." His dad stuck out his hand. Brent shook it as his dad pulled him in for a big hug.

That conversation had replayed in Brent's mind multiple times since.

Brent finished his first circuit and moved on to another one when Andrea entered using her walker. "You weren't going to use the bike, were you?" Andrea asked as she made her way through the door.

"Nope, and if I were, I'd do something else. Look at you. You've gotten a little quicker with that walker. How do you feel?"

"Like a tortoise." Everyone chuckled.

Continuing to spot her on the right side, Bob assured her it was normal. "I had another patient who'd had the same surgery as you. After one month, he was just starting to move with his walker, never mind using a stationary bike."

Brent liked the way Andrea's face beamed at the compliment. He hadn't expected anything less; Andrea worked hard for what she wanted. During their late-night talks, she told him her life verse was Colossians three: seventeen. "And whatever you do in word or deed, do everything in the name of the Lord, Jesus, giving thanks to God the Father through him."

"Before I forget, your mom called. They are coming over later than expected. They ran into old friends and want to have lunch with them today."

Brent looked pleased. "Great, we can have lunch together. I want to discuss something with you."

When she entered the kitchen, he'd just finished making Cobb salads for him and Andrea. "Where's your walker?"

"Taking a break. The walker and bike kicked my butt this morning. Besides, Bob suggested I have a spotter instead of trying these things alone.

"I can help you if you want," Brent stated, hoping she took him up on his suggestion.

She looked at Brent with a questioning eye and half a smile.

Man, is she cute. The way her lip curls a little. Brent steadied his emotions and sat her salad down on the table. Before he shared an opportunity with her, he needed to know where her head was regarding him.

"No dressing, right?" Brent brought their salads and a couple of bottles of water to the table.

Shaking her head, Andrea met his eyes. "No, thank you."

Brent placed his hand on top of Andrea's. He gave thanks for the food and their time together. He cleared his throat. "You never said anything about what I told you yesterday."

The deer in the headlights look she gave him cut to his marrow. "Okay. I'll take that as my answer."

"No, no. no." Andrea set her hand on his forearm. "You shocked me yesterday when you said it. I wondered if you misspoke or something, but I guess not." He loved her nervous chuckle.

"Definitely not." Brent held her gaze until she spoke.

"I'm afraid to let myself fall any further for you." Andrea took a sip of her water before she continued.

"Ah, *any further,* so that means you *have* fallen. I knew you couldn't resist all this." Brent held his arms out wide.

Andrea shook her head and laughed, filling his heart with heat.

"You'll wake up one day, realize I'm weighing you down, and leave. I just don't know if I can handle that again." Andrea laid her heart on the table.

Brent rubbed his palm against his cheek. "I hear what you're saying. I'm nervous, too. We both have baggage, but if we're unwilling to take a risk, we could miss out on a great experience with each other."

They ate a few bites of their salad in silence. Brent wasn't sure if what he said would make a difference until...

"I'm falling for you, too," Andrea said softly.

A triumphant grin filled Brent's face. His heart pounded. His body temperature increased instantly. "Really?"

"You seem surprised," Andrea smirked. "Where'd Mr. Confident go?"

"When it comes to your feelings for me, I have to fake it until I make it." He gripped his chin. "It does make it easier to talk to you about something else, though."

"Shoot."

"Joe and I are going to a conference the last week in November through the third week in December."

"That's one long conference." Andrea croaked, taking another bite of her salad.

Brent explained, "Whenever we go to a conference, if it's a place worth staying, we extend our time for a vacation. Since the Park is open from the third week in March until November, we don't have much time to get away. The conference is only a week."

"This must be a great place if you're extending your time that much." Andrea insisted.

He confirmed her thought. Running his fingers through her hair, he continued, "I'd like you to join us." Brent refrained from telling her that Joe was asking Donna to go at this very minute, too. Before offering that information, he needed to know she would go to be with him.

Smirking playfully, Andrea rested her elbow on the table. 'I guess that depends on where you're headed." "If it's a tropical location, so I can escape the cold air that has forced its way into New England, I think that would work."

"If I told you Minnesota, would that be a deal breaker?" Brent questioned.

Watching Andrea muse for a moment kept Brent on edge. *Does she enjoy watching me squirm?* Rubbing a hand through his hair, she finally divulged her thoughts.

"While I'd love a little, hot, secluded island for obvious reasons," Andrea placed her fingers gently on Brent's forearm. "I'd be open to other locations if you're going to be there."

Brent's eyebrows shot up quickly, then dropped just as fast. His heart welcomed her announcement. "Oh really!"

He recalled his sister telling him she got butterflies when Jerry Bronson asked her to the dance. He didn't have butterflies. He had an air current strong enough for a full-grown eagle to soar in his lower belly. He couldn't take any longer. Brent leaned closer, placing a row of kisses down her cheek. He hovered over her lips briefly, just long enough to fish his fingers through the hair at her nape and pull her into his waiting lips. "Now I kind of wish we were going to Minnesota," Brent said with a sly smirk.

"The conference is in Hawaii," Brent spoke quietly next to her face.

"Ahhhhh, for real?" Brent jumped back in his seat. Andrea's smile reached her ears. "I'd love to go with you. Thank you for asking me."

Brent's mind drifted to a tropical ocean, Hawaii. The famous trade winds blow softly, causing small waves in the blue-green water of Waikiki Beach to rise and crash down at the shoreline. Then, sitting in the sand, Brent visioned Andrea, suntaning on the shore. The idea of them rubbing suntan lotion on each other's back made him shiver.

Then, all too sudden, Andrea's smile faded, and Brent's heart dropped faster than one of those amusement park thrill drop rides.

"What's wrong?" Brent rested his hand on her cheek; she leaned into it, enjoying his tender touch.

"I can't get around a beach in that," Andrea pointed over her shoulder to her wheelchair." He saw the life sucked right out of her.

Without hesitating, Brent kissed her on the other cheek, "I'll carry you," his face grave as a heart attack."

"You can't carry me all vacation," Andrea countered. "Besides, I have PT every day."

Adrenaline filled him as he thought about having this woman in his arms. "I can carry you anywhere." He gently kissed her lips. Will you let me carry you, please?"

"You can't carry me when you're in the conference, but I guess we can figure things out as we go." Andrea's shoulders reached her ears. "I am so excited." She clapped her hands together as her face lit up.

Brent nonchalantly stuck his fork into his salad. "I forgot to mention that Donna is going too." Screams pierced his ears again. "Man, you have a great set of lungs, Woman." This time, he prepared himself by covering his ears. "I've already spoken to Bob. He has a buddy in Hawaii who is a therapist. He's agreed to treat you every day at the hotel's gym while we're away."

The scream wasn't as loud. This time, pure adoration and appreciation filled her face. "You really thought of everything so I could go with you." She reached out her hand and softly touched his face. "Thank you."

Brent didn't care what he had to do. He'd carry Andrea everywhere for the rest of their lives. She had captured his heart, and he wasn't concerned about getting it back.

Chapter 21

♥

Andrea's favorite Thanksgiving was always because she played games all day long with her parents. They weren't big on the major food production. Instead, they made a sweet potato casserole, a tiny turkey, buttercup squash, and chocolate pudding for dessert.

This year, Stacy and Kaleb, Brent's parents, were visiting. They were all about a huge Thanksgiving feast. As far as Andrea knew, Donna and Joe were eating at her parents' house for lunch and then going to Joe's parents' house for dinner, but Donna had been very vague with her details.

"Andrea, dear, where can I find the masher?"

"Um... I don't have one. I do have an emersion blender, though. Let me get it for you." Andrea started to roll toward the long cabinet.

"Let me get it." Stacy rushed toward Andrea. "Which drawer is it in?" Andrea pointed and gave Brent's overprotective mom a fake smile.

"Honey, Andrea takes care of herself daily; you don't need to baby her." Kaleb tried to get his wife to stop fussing over

Andrea, and she greatly appreciated the sentiment, smiling at Brent's dad.

She met Andrea's eyes. "Oh, I'm so sorry. You can function without me, can't you?" Andrea felt sad for the woman. It was apparent she missed taking care of others.

"I can, but if it really makes you that happy, I'll let you do it all. I will say I'd rather help with the cooking instead of the cleaning." The trio laughed together.

Brent entered the room and crossed his arms over his chest. "What did I miss?" The way he stood spoke to her chest. Her heart pounded. Hot blood rushed through her vital organs like a rapid ride.

She took a breath. "Looks like you're on clean-up duty," Andrea smirked.

He shrugged. "I guess that's the way it works. Dad, why don't you let the ladies finish up? You and I will clean up afterward."

Once the men left the room, Andrea picked up where Kaleb left off, peeling potatoes. "Do we have to peel the whole bag?"

"I always have, then there's leftovers for a couple of days," Stacy explained.

Andrea quietly peeled the entire five pounds. Stacy seemed uncomfortable around her today. It made Andrea's insecurity spike. They'd spent a few hours together every day since they'd arrived; why would today be any different?

"It's nice to see Brent so happy. He hasn't truly smiled, like he does now, since Samantha died. Thank you for bringing the life back into his soul."

A burst of excitement erupted in Andrea's chest. *Had she really done that for Brent?* She didn't think so, but moms know their children best, right? With this new insight, Andrea might be able to let her guard down a little more.

"Have you ever considered getting married?" Stacy pulled that question out of the thin air...very thin. In fact, Andrea couldn't breathe. Her lungs constricted. She swallowed and now was choking on her spit. *Seriously?*

"I am not convinced that marriage is in the cards for me, but that's a nice fantasy." Andrea grabbed a cup and filled it with water from the front of the refrigerator.

Despite making progress since her surgery, she still noticed the areas where her disability was a disadvantage. Going to Hawaii would have many struggles, such as the plane ride, the sand, and working with a different physical therapist, but she'd already agreed to go. Worry ate at her insides.

Stacy had stopped what she was doing and focused on Andrea. "Don't think like that. You are a catch, and I bet someone smart will snatch you up before you know it."

She watched Stacy peel and cut the squash. Tears welled up in her eyes as she replaced the woman in front of her with her own mother's face. This was only the second Thanksgiving without her parents. Andrea had walked through the dark tunnel for the last twenty-one months; she prayed the light would overpower the darkness soon.

"Andrea," Stacy's brows lifted. "Are you okay, dear?" She placed her hand over Andrea's. "You were miles away."

"It's hard without my parents." Andrea wiped at a rene-gade tear she hadn't expected. "Sorry," She wiped her tears away.

Andrea had lost her whole family during that accident. She couldn't even imagine what being part of a family looked like nowadays.

Stacy shook her head, half chuckling under her breath. "You have nothing to be sorry for. Don't tell, but I spent the first hour of my day crying for Samantha."

The ladies shared a tear–filled hug.

Sure, Andrea felt awful not having her parents, but that was expected in the universe - kids lose their parents and mourn them the rest of their lives in whatever way they see fit.

But what Stacy endured - the loss of a child - was not supposed to happen. At least that was what her mom al-ways told her anyway, and her mom had never steered her wrong.

After stuffing their bellies, Andrea and Stacy relaxed on the couch while Brent and Kaleb cleaned everything up. A sigh escaped her lungs. "I haven't eaten that much at one time for as long as I can remember." Andrea rested her forearm across her stomach.

"You barely ate a full plate." Stacy crowed.

The two women watched an episode of *Three's Company* because that was what she had in the Blu-Ray player. Stacy had watched the show when she was younger and reminisced throughout the episode.

Not long after, the guys were finished cleaning up and joined them in the living room. An image pulled at her heart. It was much of what happens now— her and Brent resting on the couch every night after eating and cleaning up, his arm draped over her, and him stealing kisses whenever there would be a commercial.

"What are you thinking?" Brent whispered into her ear so his parents couldn't hear, not that they would have since their attention was on the shenanigans happening on the television.

Heat filled her face. She couldn't tell him she envisioned them as a married couple, like his parents, enjoying life's simple pleasures. "About how lovely it is relaxing with you on the couch." That was the truth; she just left out the details.

Inwardly, Andrea was suffocating. She thought being able to walk again would lift her spirits, but it didn't yet. Maybe her wheelchair didn't have anything to do with Kyle leaving. Perhaps he just used that as an excuse. Why hadn't she thought of that before now? Great, now his rejection had everything to do with her and not her disability.

After wasting too much time thinking about that unpleasant thought, Andrea let her mind think about the present. Brent's warm hand rested on her shoulder. His thigh pressed up against hers. She wondered if her tablet could tell her legs to retract toward her belly, letting her knees hang over his thighs. Then she could turn into him and rest on his chest. Sadly, that involved too much work.

From the beginning, Brent had been honest with her, or so it seemed. He didn't care about her being in a chair unless she wanted to zip line alone. The thought of their rocky start made her chuckle internally since they'd come so far. Andrea stopped denying that she'd fallen for Brent. He'd declared the same.

"What are you smiling about?" Brent whispered in her ear again.

"Just about how we met."

"That doesn't paint either of us in a pretty light," Brent said as he shook his head. "I like where we are right now."

"Hey, you two, what are you whispering about?"

"Stace, leave the kids alone," Kaleb chastised his wife. That comment earned him double smiles - one from Brent and one from Andrea.

"We're heading to the airport in the morning; what should we do our last night?"

"Mom, you're not suggesting what I think you are, are you?" Brent sounded slightly annoyed. "Whenever it doesn't go your way, it isn't pretty."

"Very True," Kaleb agreed.

"Come on, guys." Just one game of Parcheesi. I won't ask for a second game ... even if I lose." Stacy slapped her palms together like she was praying or begging. Andrea wondered how long it would take before Kaleb and Brent gave in to her pleading.

"I'll agree to one game, but Andrea may not want to endure your ruthless board game competitiveness." Brent shook his head and motioned his finger across his throat like his mother would kill over a board game. She didn't believe this remarkable woman could be so ruthless.

"Four, five, six. Aw, I'm sorry, I'll put him in your home." Stacy picked up one of Kaleb's pawns and slapped it back at the start. "Now I get to move twenty." She spent a good forty-five seconds determining which of her pawns to move. It just so happened that one of her pawns was exactly twenty away from her middle winning area. "Nineteen, twenty." A beaming smile filled the woman's face. She now had three pawns in the winner's square in the middle. "Now I can move him ten."

"Stacy, I am in awe of your ability to control a Parcheesi game. However, I think your husband and son are right; you need help." Andrea burst out laughing while Stacy's sing-song voice finished moving her final pawn closer to her winning spot.

After Stacy creamed them in the game, his parents decided to head out. "Thank you so much for letting us have Thanksgiving with you. Andrea, I hope to see you again really soon."

Andrea noticed a look between Brent and his mother, but she didn't make a big deal about it, knowing it was probably just her imagination working over time.

Once the hugging ceased and Brent walked his parents to their car, he returned, plopping on the couch beside her.

"Sorry, my mom can be a bit overzealous when it comes to games of any kind."

"It's okay. I had fun." The only thing on overdrive right now was Andrea's heart. From the moment Brent sat down, it beat faster, like the winning horse at the Kentucky Derby. He had to know how he affected her.

Andrea opened her mouth slightly to say something, but Brent surprised her by capturing her lips with his. She parted her lips ever so slightly and let out a soft moan that encouraged Brent to devour her lips.

Mmm, He is such a good kisser. Andrea moved her arms around his neck, allowing Brent to pull Andrea in tighter. His hands roamed the length of her back, leaving a wake of hot chocolate goodness.

When they pulled apart, Brent rested his head on her forehead, taking a minute to catch their breath. "Should we get to bed? We'll have jet lag in a few short days; maybe we can curb it now.

Doubtful. But knowing that Hawaii was on the horizon made her giddy. *Don't think about all the things that could go wrong, Andrea. Enjoy your time with Brent in paradise.*

Chapter 22

O F ALL THE PLACES she thought she'd be right now, Hawaii was not one of them. At home, working with the physical therapist, maybe, but not in this elaborate gym overlooking the Pacific Ocean. Jeff, her temporary physical therapist, was a killer. Bob tried to warn her, but she thought he might have been exaggerating. *Nope!*

After one hour of working with him, she found her chair to be a wonderful respite. To think, she referred to it as her prison not so long ago. It was funny how God could change one's perspective based on one's experiences. The mere thought of walking right now paralyzed her.

"I don't think I'll be able to swim this afternoon; thank you very much." Andrea razzed Jeff for working her so hard.

"You'll thank me in about a month or two when all you need is your walker. Then, if you keep working as hard as you did today, another three or four months after that, it'll be you and your tablet, no walker, no chair. You have the determination to walk again."

"Thank you." Andrea did mean it. She knew he only asked her to do things he thought she could based on completing the tasks he'd given her.

"Besides, you'll recover from this morning's work in a little while. Swimming would be a great plan for today. It will loosen your muscles and get you ready for tomorrow." He winked at her as he exited the gym.

"You better run." Andrea chuckled as she hollered the empty threat toward the open door.

Andrea hadn't been swimming in the ocean since before her accident. Yeah, she'd been kayaking, and Brent had taken her swimming at the college last week, but swimming in the ocean versus a pool was a beast. Nerves ratcheted up in her belly. She silently prayed for strength as she wheeled herself out of the gym and to the lobby to meet Donna.

The conference would end at noon today, leaving them the rest of the day for a surprise excursion. Andrea could hardly contain the excitement racing through her. They had every adventure imaginable at their fingertips. She equated this moment to Christmas day for a child.

Despite becoming more robust and mobile, she noticed her entire body was sore. Every muscle in her upper body was being pushed to its limits, and in the lower extremities, they were screaming for help. Brent had massaged her shoulders and upper back every night since they'd arrived.

"Parasailing?" Donna questioned. "I told Joe I could do that since he'd be beside me."

"Snorkeling, or maybe we're going to the Polynesian Cultural Center." Andrea clapped her hands together. "That's what I told Brent I'd like to do. He didn't complain when he learned about the ladies from Tahiti who show guests how to dance." Andrea smiled and rolled her eyes.

"Hello, ladies." Brent pressed his lips to Andrea's while Joe kissed Donna's temple. "Ready to go?"

"Where are you taking us?" Andrea smirked and crossed her arms over her chest playfully.

Brent studied Andrea, then Donna. Joe nodded his head. "We're going zip-lining."

"Oh, no, I'm not." Donna turned on her heels and got three steps away before Joe brought her back. "You'll be with me. It will be okay."

Andrea's arm fell loosely on her lap. "This is an interesting turn of events. Before, I had to fight tooth and nail for months just to zip line. Why the change of heart?"

"You're not fighting to go by yourself. It's interesting how that works. When you're safe, I don't have a problem." His tone was more sarcastic than she'd ever heard before. The raspiness made up for it.

"Well, if I'd known that's all it would take..." Andrea smiled at Brent as she let her words die off.

During the entire ride there, Joe, Brent, and Andrea convinced Donna to try it again now that she'd done it once. When they arrived, Andrea's pulse raced. Brent had an excellent establishment for their rural area, but this place was a theme park of zip lines. Heaven on earth. That's the only way to describe this place.

Andrea was impressed with Joe, Mr. Adventure himself. He started at the beginner lines to keep his promise to

Donna and be right by her side. Her heart melted even more when Brent did the same thing. They started at the intermediate lines comparable to the one she completed at Brent's a few months back.

Andrea and Brent both made it across the first two sections without trouble. These sections were longer and more strenuous on her arms than at Brent's, or her arms were just tired from all the work she'd been doing in physical therapy. She had taken a brief break on each platform before starting a new section. Even with those rest periods, they were making good time. Brent looked at his watch - two fifteen. "I hope Joe and Donna are having a good time."

"Me too. I must admit I was touched by how Joe paid attention to Donna's feelings and her anxiety."

"I appreciate my friendship with Joe. He was always there for me, literally since Kindergarten."

Andrea cooed. "That's really cute." She rested her palm on his forearm. "I appreciate you because you did the same thing Joe did. I know you'd rather be done with the advanced course, not just starting it. Thank you for being thoughtful." She loved the way his cheeks got a bright pink. "You could have let the employees take care of me. Instead, here you are, right by my side."

"Always." He placed a tender kiss on her lips.

All Andrea and Brent needed to do for the first section of the advance rope was cross the rope net, hook on the zip line, and zoom down. That sounds easy, but the rope net had bars farther apart and more challenging grips. Andrea was tired. She hadn't done a course this hard since before her accident. Her muscles were raw.

She prayed quickly, asking the Lord to get her safely to the zip line. In front of her, she saw Brent's shoulder and arm muscles tense and loosen as he maneuvered across the net. The platform, less than twenty yards away, called her name. When Andrea grabbed onto the middle rope, she felt a twinge in her right shoulder and instantly lost grip on that side.

"Andrea!" Brent exclaimed. "Are you okay?"

"My right shoulder gave out," Andrea yelled in return, dangling from one arm, replicating a monkey. She watched Brent make his way back toward her.

"You're fine. I'm coming." Brent assured her. The extra workers the manager put in place for Andrea's safety were also heading to help.

Andrea tried to stop them. "No, I'll be okay." Nobody listened to her. She was glad since her left arm had begun throbbing.

Brent reached Andrea first. He had her strap the other end of the protective belt they required her to wear around Brent's waist while he held onto her with one arm.

Once she finished securing herself to Brent, she wrapped her arms around his neck. Brent reached the platform with ease.

Sitting beside one another on the plank, Brent rubbed Andrea's shoulder, "Are you okay? By this time, three workers were asking her the same question.

No.

Andrea hesitated. "I'm fine. Sorry." She stared at her legs.

"For what?" Brent asked, shocked.

"I put you in danger because of my desire to push myself." Andrea rested her hand on his thigh.

Brent lifted Andrea's chin. "You are amazingly strong. This is not an easy course. Trouble didn't find you until the end."

"Thank you for helping me through that." Andrea kissed Brent on the cheek. She looked at the workers and apologized to them as well before they retreated.

A grin larger than all the islands combined spread across Brent's face. "If you're going to kiss me every time I help you, I might have to help you a lot more.

Brent hopped up. He picked Andrea up and placed her on the wooden seat to prepare her for flight. He hooked her to the cable after he hooked his. "I'll see you down there. This is it. Are you all set?"

"Yup," Andrea said, tugging on her strap.

"I'll be waiting to help you off." Looking at the worker. "You ready to start the timer." the young woman nodded. "See you in three and a half minutes. Whoo-hoo." Brent roared when he leaped off the platform.

The girl checked Andrea's connection one last time. "Thirty seconds, and then you're up. Are you ready?"

"Definitely."

When the timer beeped at them, the young girl bid her farewell as she spotted Andrea as she exited her mark. Once again, Andrea felt free. Except this time, the freeing feeling had nothing to do with her inability to walk; it came from within. Her heart felt free to love and trust. Brent was worth a risk...she loved him.

The couples enjoyed dinner and had since gone their separate ways to savor some alone time. Andrea and Brent were strolling around the hotel complex. It was massive. The different shops and restaurants were intriguing. She would have preferred walking along the shoreline, but she was not there yet. Brent offered to rent a wheelchair that rolled in the sand, but she declined. She was tired and knew they'd turn in quickly.

As if on cue, Brent yawned. "We have an early conference time tomorrow. Do you mind if we call it a night?"

"Of course not."

They made their way to the Tower Hotel. Brent pressed the up button on the elevator. Inside, she pushed the circle with the number seventeen printed in black. She never liked being anywhere other than the first floor for evacuation purposes, but she'd risk it here.

The view of the ocean took all her cares away. Every morning, Donna had bolted to the bakery in the village area for breakfast bagels. Then, they ate their breakfast together on their balcony. Best time ever!

The guys had adjoining rooms, which she liked for safety purposes. When they reached her door, he asked, " What was your favorite part of the day?"

Andrea blushed as Brent wrapped his arms around her waist and under her legs. He held her inches from his face, patiently waiting for her answer.

Andrea arched up, grabbed his black and white hooded sweatshirt strings, and tugged him even closer. "You." She planted a kiss on his lips that was meant to be a quick goodnight kiss, but she held it longer than anticipated. Brent took over, gently navigating his lips over hers with such precision. He knew the route he wanted to take.

Andrea pressed her hand on his chest and gently pulled away, "If you are trying to keep me from sleeping, we may have an issue. Jeff is a killer." Andrea joked. Kissing Brent had become her favorite pastime. Brent smiled at her and settled her back in her chair, held his hand out for her key card from her hand, and opened her door.

After saying good night again, the door shut with a loud bang. Andrea didn't move for at least thirty seconds. She heard the beep through the wall as Brent entered his and Joe's room. Then that door banged shut, too.

For the first time since her accident, Andrea's heart had done the opposite of the door. Instead of banging shut with a force that would scare Thor, it had rolled out the red carpet and welcomed Brent to become a permanent resident.

Chapter 23

♥

THE FIRST FEW DAYS of the conference were a blur. While Brent and Joe had learned invaluable information they were eager to implement in the spring, he was more excited about meeting Andrea every afternoon when the session ended.

Today, he'd spoken to his dad on the phone to share his plans with his parents. His dad's tee time kept the conversation short.

In an effort to connect with his dad as a teenager, Brent had asked his dad to teach him how to play golf. It didn't take long before Brent started to outscore his dad, creating competing monsters in each of them.

After Brent and his dad reunited during their most recent visit, they let a little bit of their pride dissipate as they apologized for allowing their grief to be more potent than their father-and-son connection.

They'd made up for lost time by golfing despite the chilly fall temperatures. Brent had received his love for adventure from his mom but his competitiveness from his dad. Brent wouldn't choose to golf on his own, but that is what he and his dad did to bond.

Brent and his dad played four times on this trip. He'd beaten his dad the first three times, but the fourth time, Brent had let his dad win. Brent hadn't made any excuses like his shoulder hurt or anything like his dad had the last three events. Instead, Brent congratulated his dad and slapped him on the back. Watching his dad beam, Brent felt peace flow through him.

It was freeing talking to his dad. No more built-up anger or resentment, but respect and love. His dad broke into his thoughts. "I'm happy for you, Son. Let your mother and I know how it goes.

"Thanks, Dad. Talk soon. Bye."

This time, Brent and Joe met the ladies at a shellfish shack, where they had shrimp skewers and purple rice. "Hmmm. This is delicious." Andrea took another bite.

"Sorry, the conference was extra long today. I missed you." Brent said as he leaned in closer, his lips nipping her ear.

"What they say is true, huh? Andrea asked, pulling back to look him in the eyes.

Brent missed her skin already, "What's that?"

"Absence makes the heart grow fonder." Andrea smiled, tracing his lips with her finger.

Brent chuckled, "Definitely," he murmured, capturing her lips. When he dragged his lips from hers, he downed another bite of the rice. "How did PT go today?"

"Jeff said that my range of motion was improving. He believes it's the warmer weather. He added hip bridges to my stretch routine. I still have a long road ahead of me, but at least I'm headed in the right direction."

Yes, they both were headed in the right direction. He couldn't pull his eyes away from her angelic face. Gazing at her full lips left him desiring another kiss. He didn't hesitate.

"Wow," she murmured as he gently tugged on her bottom lip.

His gaze held hers while he stood. Then he took their trash to the barrel. When he returned, Brent was in front of her chair with his arms around her waist. He loved the squeal that left her mouth when he lifted her to his chest and gave her one of the deepest kisses they had ever shared. Breaking away, he felt her heart beating like the thunderstorm they'd experienced on the island yesterday. He couldn't wait to surprise her.

He'd had all day to get himself ready for this moment. They had rented a car to tour Oahu, thinking it would settle his nerves. It hadn't. Once they'd finished their shrimp and rice lunch, they'd visited a farm that sold macadamia nuts with many different flavorings.

"Hmm, try this," Andrea said as she passed Brent a honey-roasted one.

After chewing slowly, tilting his head side to side, and lifting his eyes to the ceiling like he needed to contemplate, he finally answered. "That's pretty good." Their next stop was the North Shore. Two weeks from now, the month-long surfing championship would begin.

"Awe-inspiring waves here this time of year," Andrea said to the open air since the rest of the gang took a little stroll along the shore. This would have upset her just a few months ago. Not today. The salty air filled her lungs, and the sight alone left her peaceful.

Brent returned first with a plumeria for Andrea. "I beautiful flower for a gorgeous woman." He gently pushed the stem into Andrea's hair and kissed her on the cheek.

"Thank you." Andrea smoothed the petal between her thumb and forefinger. "Was this my surprise?"

A little chuckle escaped from Brent's lungs. "You're not impressed with this, eh?"

"This is great. I just hoped we would spend more time together." He loved how Andrea's cheeks turned slightly pink when she worried she'd said too much.

"Same. Our time will come. Don't you worry; this is not your surprise." Brent kissed her noticeably warm cheeks. "Great. Here come Joe and Donna. We're going back to the village to start your surprise."

Despite the relatively short drive back to the hotel, the sun started to set by the time Brent pulled into their destination.

"Wait here. I'll be right back." Brent rushed off with Joe and Donna.

Deep breaths. Please, God, I want your will to be done, but I want it to go my way, too. Help me to have peace that passes understanding if it doesn't end in my favor. I trust you.

"May I be of assistance to you, Ma'am?" Brent asked as he positioned a chair he rented from the front desk to the door he just opened. His face cooled when the breeze from Andrea's air conditioner on full bore struck him in the face. *Ah, thank you, Lord. That feels great.* It wasn't that warm outside, but his insides felt like Pahoehoe, a type of lava flow. One of the hotel greeters told Brent it's pronounced pah-hoy-hoy, which was well-known in Hawaii, even worldwide, to those studying volcanoes. What would they be called? Volcanologists?

Brent didn't know, and he really didn't care. A brain fog inhibited his ability to think of anything except the next thirty minutes. Joe got him all worked up and nervous, so everything was amplified for him.

Apprehension filled Brent as he trudged through the sand, pushing Andrea to the spot he meticulously picked out the night they had arrived in Hawaii. The wheelchair he rented to go through sand made his plan possible, but Brent wouldn't call it easy. His heart beat faster, and even though he exerted more physical energy pushing the chair in the sand, he knew, without a doubt, that the work had nothing to do with that.

The concierge made it sound easy to put these chairs through the sand. Not so much. However, it would be worth his energy if Brent gets his way. He'd booked a cabana for the entire day since he knew finding a secluded spot on Waikiki Beach would be nearly impossible.

When they arrived at the cabana, Brent lifted Andrea onto one of the lounge chairs. The table in between the two chairs had a tray of the foods Andrea had been eating every day since she'd arrived. Donna had been a significant help in going to the hotel deli, ordering, and setting up for them. Brent noticed Andrea didn't eat much differently on vacation than at home: hard-boiled eggs, strawberries, almonds, and one bite-sized sushi roll.

When Brent set Andrea on the chair, he took up the space next to her hip and laced his fingers through hers. His hands were clammy.

Why am I so nervous? Just ask her. The worst she can say is no. Dear God, please don't let that happen.

He gently ran his thumb across her smooth, silky skin. He expected that. What he hadn't counted on were the words that slipped from Andrea's mouth. "I think I'm in love with you."

She'd whispered so low that Brent took an extra moment to process, ensuring he heard her correctly. "You think?" Brent choked out the words, caressing her arm with the thumb of his other hand.

"Yeah, I know I am truly, madly, deeply in love with you, but I've been afraid to tell you, thinking I might scare you off. For that reason, I keep fighting the feelings. This is the first time I've admitted them aloud."

Thank you, Lord! You know how to help a guy!

Brent bolted to his knees, never letting go of Andrea's hand, but now he just held her fingers. He kissed the back of her hand to give his heart a moment to get his nerves under control. "You are the best thing that has *ever* happened to me. He accentuated *ever* in a deep, bold tone and smiled as he wrapped a loose tendril behind her ear. I want to watch every sunset with you for the rest of my life. Granted, the sunsets in Hawaii are deeper and more romantic than anywhere in the world, but I will do whatever it takes to share as many sunsets as possible."

Brent cringed as Andrea stared at him like a deer caught in a headlight. Unable to move, look away, or even think. It was like she was searching deep in his soul as he spoke intently.

"I know I love you, too." Brent held up a princess cut, platinum gold ring with three small diamonds on either side of the center rock. She didn't know where it had come from. Andrea's eyes raced back and forth between Brent's face and the ring. He saw her chest rising and falling in big, heavy motions, her hand jerked to cover her unhinged jaw.

Brent wiped his brow before sweat landed in his eye. "Would you, Andrea Williams, do me the sincere honor of marrying me so I can love you every day of my life, wake up next to you every morning, and cherish you in every way a man should cherish his wife?"

Andrea screamed *YES*, but only in her head. Sound refused to come out of her opened mouth. She used her free hand to fan herself, making Brent smile. All she could do was smile and shake her head vigorously.

"Yes?!" Brent questioned. Then she found her voice.

"Absolutely, yes, yes, yes!" Brent slipped the ring on her finger. Leaning her back on the lounge chair, Brent's upper body pinned her in place. He drank her in, kissing her more profoundly than he ever had before. Andrea hadn't even known that was possible.

"Did Donna know this was happening?" Andrea questioned.

"Um, that depends on if you're mad or not." Brent smiled cautiously.

"Why would I be upset? I'd thank her if she knew and helped make it happen." Andrea said, caressing Brent's arm. Her hands slid up his neck, pulling him back in. Her hands felt like heaven on his skin. Elation filled Brent's chest.

The warmth of her breath mingled with his. His pulse quickened. This woman had agreed to be his wife. The idea of kissing her every day for the rest of his life filled him with joy. Her silky hands ran along his back and biceps, giving him a glimpse of eternity. Lying on the chair with her, he closed the gap between them. Squeezing her waist, he gently pulled her toward him. Their make-out session was interrupted when a rustling outside the canvas bungalow caught Brent's attention.

Sitting back up, he hollered, "Come on in, guys; she said yes."

Donna squealed close to the same pitch as Andrea before he saw her jumping up and down and clapping in the entryway of the cabana. "I'm so excited for you guys."

Brent spent the rest of the evening holding his fiancé's hand and staring at her until she playfully shoved him. He'd finally found the woman of his dreams. The one he'll grow old with, the one that, even if she starts walking again, he'll carry her anywhere.

Chapter 24

♥

The couple's time in Hawaii seemed more like three days than three weeks. She'd missed Bruno so much that she sat beside him on the couch all day since she'd picked him up from the doggy daycare. He'd been well cared for for the last twenty-one days, but the distance helped her see how much she loved Bruno.

Andrea let out a slow breath. Her life had changed drastically in the last thirty days. Medically, she was trudging along the road to being able to walk again. She'd gotten engaged - something she never thought would happen after her accident. They compromised on when they'd get married but had yet to set a date. Brent wanted to get married in Hawaii, but she wanted to wait a while to see if she could walk down the aisle instead of rolling.

On the sitcom she was watching with Bruno, the family enjoyed a day of snorkeling together. That reminded Andrea of their last adventure in Hawaii.

Brent had found a company willing to dedicate an employee to working with Andrea so she could enjoy the experience, too. They hit it off with Jon, the only helpful employee.

Grateful. That wasn't a strong enough word to express her emotions for the man. He'd offered to work on his only day off. Andrea would have had to wait back in the shop while everyone else snorkeled if he hadn't.

Brent offered to pay the employee privately, but the boss, who seemed more like a dictator than a person someone would choose to work for, refused, stating that he would pay the guy his regular hourly pay. This didn't feel right to Brent or Andrea. They realized that the employee was doing them a favor. Other employees had refused to come in on their day off to help her. They wanted to show sufficient gratitude, so they took matters into their own hands after the excursion to show their appreciation.

"Are you all set?" Donna and Joe came up behind Andrea.

"Absolutely, you?"

Brent finished his conversation with Jon before introducing him to Donna and Joe. "Guys, this is Jon. He'll be assisting Andrea today."

Donna, Joe, and then Andrea reached out their hands one at a time and met his hand with a firm handshake.

Andrea beamed. "It's nice to meet you, Jon. Thank you for coming in on your day off."

"No problem." He told her, "I will get you on the boat first. Are you ready?"

"Definitely," Andrea smiled.

Their two-and-a-half-hour snorkeling session was over at warp speed. A supreme professional, Jon led Andrea to the best spots to view the animals. He'd floated Andrea two feet in front of a giant sea turtle. She'd used her underwater camera to snap close-ups. She couldn't believe how massive they were.

When the boat docked at the end of the tour, Jon carried Andrea to her wheelchair. From there, Brent shook the man's hand, slipping him a hundred-dollar bill to express their gratitude.

"I couldn't have done this without you. I really appreciated your help today," Andrea said softly.

"Mahalo, Thank you!" John hugged Andrea. "You don't even know what this means to me."

They bid Jon adieu, catching up with Donna and Joe in the waiting area, where a small gift shop enticed tourists to buy shirts, hats, reef-safe sunscreen, and other souvenirs.

Andrea recalled the thoughts she had at that moment. *Maybe we should get married here.* Brent glistened in the sun. A clump of hair tossed aside hung low into his forehead. Flawless. That was the only word she thought did Brent any justice.

The doorbell pulled her back to the present. Bruno hopped off the couch. Sniffed around the bottom and then the knob. Just then, she heard, "Bruno, it's me, please open the door,"

Loud enough so her visitor could hear, Andrea spoke to Bruno. "I don't know Buddy. Should we let him in?"

"Funny. It's cold out here. Please. I have ice cream." His sing-song voice got her attention.

"Quick, let him in, Bruno."

Brent petted the dog on the head once inside the door. "Thanks, I can see how important I am."

He dropped a kiss on the top of Andrea's head. "Would you like this now, or should I put it in the freezer?"

"Freezer, please."

"This weather makes me wish we lived in Hawaii." Andrea hollered so Brent could hear her in the kitchen.

"But it wouldn't be as fun to come visit here. It's a lot of fun to visit there. With so many excursions, we'd never be bored. It would take a decade of annual trips to accomplish everything.

"True. I'd go back to see Jon and go snorkeling." Andrea said as she pulled Brent by the arm to sit next to her.

"Oh?" Brent's brows lifted, questioning her intention behind that statement.

"Not like that. He made snorkeling a great experience for me when others wouldn't. He seemed appreciative of the tip, too."

"I liked the people at Parasailing Oahu. They were just as great as Jon. It's too bad they couldn't team up together. Their customer service alone would put others out of business."

"True story."

"You know, I made that reservation before we'd even left for Hawaii." The look of shock, or maybe appreciation, warmed Brent's soul. "When you told me how much you loved parasailing, I planned to propose during our flight off the boat, but I couldn't wait." Brent grinned and shrugged his shoulders. Tears of joy wet her cheeks. Pure love for the man kneeling in front of her filled her heart.

"What's wrong?" Concern etched around his eyes.

"Nothing," Andrea sniffed, and plump tears streamed down her face. Andrea wrapped her hand around Brent's neck and gently pulled his lips toward hers. Her soft, moist lips tenderly brushed her fiancé's lips. Every wave of doubt she had ever had about this man's ability to love and care for her had dissipated. She danced her lips across his with more passion than she ever had to demonstrate her love for him.

"Are you sure you're okay?" Brent asked, pulling away slightly.

Andrea cupped Brent's face, "I am better than okay. I hope I make you even half as happy as you've made me. How soon before I can become Mrs. Brent Smith?

"You tell me." Brent lifted Andrea from her chair, kissing her cheek. "I'm ready when you are."

Andrea had thought about her fantasy wedding from the time she turned six years old. She had practiced wearing her mom's wedding shoes and pretty dresses. Her mom's wedding dress lay inactive in the back of her closet, patiently waiting for this moment. Brent had already told her that he would love to have his parents at his wedding but would marry Andrea with just a moment's notice.

Andrea beamed brighter than the falling sun, "Soon. Very soon."

Unedited Chapter 1: Let Me Marry You

♥

Hawaii – Five Months Ago

"**I** SAY WE DON'T break up."

"No?" Donna's heart skipped.

"Instead of making it a big deal, telling them we set this whole thing up, faking our relationship so they would build theirs, I think we should just let this dissolve."

Her heart plummeted. "If that's what you think is best." She thought his smile dropped a little. Then it reappeared, reminding her of the great acting he'd done the past five months, putting his friend's happiness before his own.

"Are you ready for this last excursion?"

Donna looked around at the eager faces waiting for her to answer. Her stomach curdled. Somewhere along the way, Donna had enjoyed more outdoor activities with Joe. They had been on hikes and bike rides through Baxter State

Park. He had taken her golfing and not that Namby Pamby mini-golf. Eighteen holes of authentic, traditional golf, which Donna had started to enjoy...enough to go once a week with him. Unfortunately, all of that would end soon. Knowing it would be her last with Joe, could she complete one more adventure? Besides, the look on Brent's face spoke of something more extreme than golf. Being in Hawaii, where extreme sports are born, bred, and cultivated, Donna started to sweat.

"You alright, Donna?" Brent tapped Joe's arm, forcing him to pay a little more attention to his woman, who looked whiter than a ghost, ready to topple over at any moment.

"Yeah, I think I'm sick. I should go lie down. Wake me tomorrow when you finish with your fun."

Joe grabbed her wrist before she could take two steps away. Her pulse sped up with his strong hands on her petite wrist.

Without letting go, he wrapped an arm around her waist and gently brushed his lips on her cheek. "Don't worry. I know Brent. Anything he's planned will be safe and fun." He spoke into her ear, sending shivers down her spine.

She saw Andrea watching them - *just a little more. You can play this up so no one gets hurt. No one except me.* She'd given her heart to Joe. She didn't mean to. He did this on purpose with his charming, attractive demeanor. Joe had showered her with love. The only problem, he didn't love her. She would be *dissolved* from his life just like Groot turned to dust in Rocket's arms in Infinity Wars. A movie

Joe had them watch together one night in an attempt to make it look like a legitimate relationship.

"Fine." Donna and Joe turned their bodies open to hear Brent out. Joe held onto Donna tightly, probably to prevent her from running off.

Brent's apprehension was written all over his face. He tried to explain why he made the choice he did.

"I know that Donna didn't like zip-lining. I assume being a solo event, it rattled her nerves more than anything else."

She nodded her head in agreement.

"Instead, I've chosen an activity that would require a professional with us at all times." She could tell by the look on his face that she wouldn't like this ... at all.

"I feel bad that you're nervous, Donna, but Andrea's smile makes my heart happy."

"Great. You two go enjoy the adventure." Donna took a step out of Joe's loose arms. "Joe, you're free to go too. I am perfectly fine hanging out at the pool or in the ocean.

"Being here on one of Hawaii's beautiful islands will make this the best experience you've ever had..." Brent used his marketing voice in an attempt to convince Donna to participate.

"Just spit it out, Brent." Donna chimed.

"Skydiving. We're going tandem skydiving with Sky Hawaii!"

Donna's heart raced, and her stomach fell. Joe instantly tightened his grip when her knees buckled. "I can't do that."

Andrea clapped her hands excitedly. Her smile faded, and she shared a sympathetic look with Donna.

Hadn't she been selfless enough? She didn't need more guilt. *Andrea is engaged to Brent, Joe gets to forget I ever existed, and what did I get out of this? A broken heart.* They should let her quietly bow out of this excursion. Nope, that is outside their plan.

"Tandem is much safer because the professional skydiver is strapped to the back of the jumper," Andrea said as she tried to convince Donna that she'd be okay.

Donna rolled her eyes to show her disapproval. She didn't mean to act like a rebellious teenager. If she was being honest with herself, Donna hurt. She'd let herself get sucked into this relationship, spoiling any future love prospects. Her parents always taught her to take responsibility for her actions, so she refrained from blaming Joe for being easy to fall for.

"Joe, you'll be the only one who can convince her." Andrea captured Brent's eyes and jerked her head to the side. "Let's give them some time. We'll be waiting in the car. "I hope you come with us, Donna. It won't be the same without you." Andrea kissed her hand and directed it toward her best friend.

Once Andrea and Brent were out of earshot, Donna stepped back. "Please don't try to convince me to jump out of an airplane." She crossed her arms over her chest. "I have done everything you three have asked of me the last five months. I've thrown up more in the last hundred and fifty days than I have in my entire twenty-eight years on this planet."

Joe chuckled. "You're so dramatic." He joked.

"Not really, just reporting the facts." Donna deadpanned.

We're leaving soon. Skydiving in Hawaii is … remarkable. The scenery is better than any place I've ever jumped. "I'd like to experience this with you."

Her two-faced heart melted. Donna didn't know why he'd want to experience something he considered wonderful with her if he was fine with their fake relationship just dissolving. *Lord, please protect us.*

"What do you say?" Joe urged.

"Fine, let's go." Donna hoped she didn't die.

Joe held his hand out for Donna to lace her fingers with his. The feel of his strong, calloused hands reminded her of all the adventures they'd gone on together. His upper body strength impressed her. The first time he'd taken her golfing, he wrapped his strong muscles around her from behind and coached her through her first swing.

Though she'd understood the movement and could mimic it without assistance, she'd played it up so he would continue to help her. In hindsight, she shouldn't have let her heart get involved. It would be a bald-faced lie if she said she didn't do it on purpose. Frankly, she hadn't done anything to prevent falling, so she only had herself to blame for a dissolving heart.

"Yay!" Andrea opened the door and yelled.

"She has hawk eyes. How'd she even see me? Donna lifted her palm to acknowledge her friend's excitement. "Let's get this over with."

After Donna landed from her twelve thousand foot jump, she threw up, not once or twice, but three times. Strapped to Donna's back mere seconds ago, the professional skydiver escaped a disgusting fate. Despite her body's reaction, Donna proclaimed she had fun.

Once Donna cleaned herself up, the four of them decided on a place to eat. Donna wouldn't eat unless her stomach settled considerably, but she enjoyed the camaraderie.

The guys ran into a shop, telling the women to wait where they were.

"I can't believe this is happening. I found someone to love me for me." Andrea beamed as she snatched Donna's hand.

"Of course you did." Donna embraced Andrea. "You are an amazing friend. I'm sure you'll be an amazing wife too."

"I hope so. I can be stubborn sometimes." Andrea's sly smile let Donna know that she was joking.

"You, stubborn? Nah." They both laughed.

Andrea pulled her friend to eye level. Donna bounced on the balls of her feet to capture her balance. "Have you and Joe talked about getting engaged?"

Worry filled Donna's gut. If anyone could tell when something bothered her, it was Andrea. She let out a soft sigh, trying to slow her racing heart before she answered. Unsuccessful. She wiped her clammy hands down the front of her athletic shorts.

"What aren't you telling me? Andrea questioned as she pointed out Donna's cheeks. "Your rosy cheeks and small beads of sweat forming on your face tell me you're keeping something from me."

"My *rosy cheeks and beads of sweat* are telling you that I just threw up. I'll get my color back soon," Donna countered, hoping the guys would return to put a pin in this conversation.

"Are you guys already engaged and hiding it from me because you thought I'd be upset?" Andrea brought her hands up to cover her open mouth.

Oh no. What am I supposed to say to her? Donna weaved her fingers through her short blonde bob.

"Don't get your hopes up, Andrea. I'm not ready for marriage, and neither is Joe. Heck, I may die on one of these great adventures you guys plan and never make it to thirty. Only God knows."

Whenever Donna said dramatic things, Andrea would roll her eyes. This time wasn't any different. "Why are you being so dramatic?"

"I'm in a constant state of sickness. I am not an adventurous person like the three of you. Joe may be attractive, but we are too different for this to last much longer." Donna said, fighting back tears. Her chest ached, causing her heart to shiver.

Meanwhile, Andrea reached for her friend. "I'm sorry. You were always smiling." Andrea wagged her friend's arm. "Remember when the guys returned from their Mount Washington hike? You were so excited to get Joe's text." Andrea frowned. "I didn't realize you were feeling this way. I'm sorry."

"It's just been something I thought about the last couple of days when I've puked more than I've eaten." Hopefully, she was more convincing than she felt.

The guys returned with a single rose for each of them and a promise of dinner. Brent held the door for Andrea to enter and gestured for Joe and Donna to follow.

"We'll be right in," Joe said as he turned back, face to face with Donna. "Are you doing okay?"

"Not really. I hate to sit down for dinner. There's no way I can eat a thing."

"I meant, are you okay with what we talked about?" Joe searched her eyes.

Donna wrapped her arms around her middle. "This was the plan. We did what we set out to do - Brent and Andrea gave each other a chance, fell in love, and now are engaged to be married. So it's time for us to be done or *dissolve*, as you said.

It didn't matter to Donna what word they used. It all meant the same thing - she and Joe were done with this charade. Her brain knew it. Now, someone had to tell it to her heart. Her very shattered heart.

How About a Review?

♥

YOUR FEEDBACK IS VALUABLE, so please consider sharing your thoughts. This will help other readers discover this book and my other works.

Thank you from the bottom of my heart for reading and reviewing my book(s).

<u>Amazon</u>

<u>Goodreads</u>

<u>Bookbub</u>

About the Author

Karen Tucci, a public school teacher by profession, now tutors writing students online and homeschools her two children.

A native of Maine, she has trekked miles of the Pine Tree State and visited countless others. It is through her life experiences that the basis for her romance stories develop. One of her favorite things to say when out adventuring is, "...that is definitely going in my next book!"

Fun fact: Karen had only read and wrote non-fiction growing up. It wasn't until her late twenties that she embraced the joy brought forth by doing both — reading and writing — within the different romance tropes. Now she reads at least fifteen fiction novels a month and writes daily!

Connect with Karen:

<u>Facebook Reader's Group.</u>
To find out about special deals, giveaways, and new releases, join her newsletter:
<u>https://www.trueheartromance.com</u>
<u>Instagram</u>
<u>Goodreads</u>
<u>Bookbub</u>
<u>Amazon</u>